• • • • • •

"I don't think you're too strongminded. I've just never heard a woman speak like that before."

"And it amuses you?"

"No," he said. "It intrigues me." His eyes left hers, swam down her frame, devoured her exposed leg and settled on her barefoot and perfect toes. When his gaze returned to hers, he said, "If I was your man, I wouldn't mind rubbing your feet *every night*. I don't care if you had a hard day or if you ever rubbed mine. I wouldn't mind one bit."

She sucked air between her teeth. Leo saw the muscles in her neck grow tense. Flustered, she had to lower her eyes.

She told him, "I – I think it's time for you to leave."

Leo grinned as he rose to his feet. His face and chest were warm. For the first time since he'd met her, he felt like he had the upper hand. He wasn't sure how to harness this newfound energy, but he savored the feel of it.

"Will I see you tomorrow?" he asked before turning and heading for the door.

"Yes. I'll be at your office as usual. The battle has only just begun."

She sounded like she'd regained her composure. Sure enough, when he looked back, her eyes were once again focused on his.

"Yes, it's only just begun," he agreed. He wondered if she knew he was referring to his advances as well as their fight for the mayor's office. His smile deepened as he exited her home.

• • • • • •

1

I0592877

ELECTION DAY

ELECTION DAY

Decades: A Journey of African-American Romance
1970s

KEITH THOMAS WALKER

KEITHWALKERBOOKS, INC
This is a UMS production

DECADES:
A JOURNEY OF AFRICAN AMERICAN ROMANCE

January   February   March

April   May   June

July   August   September

October   November   December

KEITHWALKERBOOKS

Publishing Company
KeithWalkerBooks, Inc.
P.O. Box 331585
Fort Worth, TX 76163

All rights reserved. Except for use in any review, the reproduction or utilization of this manuscript in whole or partial in any form by any mechanical, electronic, or other means, not known or hereafter invented, including photocopying, xerography, and recording, or in any information retrieval or storage system, is forbidden without written permission of the publisher, KeithWalkerBooks, Inc.

For information write
KeithWalkerBooks, Inc.
P.O. Box 331585
Fort Worth, TX 76163

All characters in this book have no existence outside the imagination of the author and have no relation whatsoever to anyone bearing the same name or names. They are not even distantly inspired by any individual known or unknown to the author and all incidents are pure invention.

Copyright © 2018 Keith Thomas Walker

ISBN-13 DIGIT: 978-0-9850500-3-0
ISBN-10 DIGIT: 0-985050039
Library of Congress Control Number: 2018907804
Manufactured in the United States of America

Second Edition

Visit us at www.keithwalkerbooks.com

This book is for Wayne Jordan
Still praying for your recovery

MORE BOOKS BY KEITH THOMAS WALKER

Fixin' Tyrone
How to Kill Your Husband
A Good Dude
Riding the Corporate Ladder
The Finley Sisters' Oath of Romance
Blow by Blow
Jewell and the Dapper Dan
Harlot
Plan C (And More KWB Shorts)
Dripping Chocolate
The Realest Ever
Jackson Memorial
Sleeping With the Strangler
Life After
Blood for Isaiah
Brick House
Brick House 2
One on One
Brick House 3
Jackson Memorial 2
Backslide
Threesome
Backslide 2
Threesome 2

NOVELLAS

Might be Bi Part One
Harder
Primal Part One
The Realest Christmas Ever
Hotline Fling

POETRY COLLECTION

Poor Righteous Poet

FINLEY HIGH SERIES

Prom Night at Finley High
Fast Girls at Finley High
Bullies at Finley High

Visit keithwalkerbooks.com for information about these and upcoming titles from KeithWalkerBooks

ACKNOWLEDGMENTS

Of course I would like to thank God, first and foremost, for giving me the creativity and drive to pursue my dreams and the understanding that I am nothing without Him. I would like to thank my mother for always pushing me to be the best I can be. I would like to thank Janae Hafford for being the best advisor, supporter and little sister a brother could ever have.

I would also like to thank (in no particular order) Beulah Neveu, Deloris Harper, Denise Fizer, Michele Halsey Hallahan, Priscilla C. Johnson, Kim Tanner, Tia Kelly, Edwina Putney, Melissa Carter, Cathy Atchison, Lanita Irvin, Ramona Weathersbee, Cynthia Antoinette Taylor, Jason Owens, Ramona Brown, Johnathan Royal, Sharon Blount, BRAB Book Club, and Uncle Steven Thomas, one love. I'd like to thank everyone who purchased and enjoyed one of my books. Everything I do has always been to please you. I know there are folks who mean the world to me that I'm failing to mention. I apologize ahead of time. Rest assured I'm grateful for everything you've done for me!

CHAPTER ONE
I. M. TERRELL

Incompetence
Insolence
Don't even think of escaping
Because the slave patrols have hounds
And your sweat is a fragrance
And your tears are so tasty
In these woods, there's no safety
And no witnesses to lynchings
Or you're returned to your master
And sold down the river

Emancipation brought elation
Yet sedition and resistance
Ran rampant down south
Forty acres?
Negro, please
Not a dime – not one inch!
Of this land
Where you toiled
Built this nation with no wages
Segregated
Alienated

A century later
You can find them
Descendants of slaves
Miseducated
Unanswered prayers
Deprived but grateful
Far from the civil
They live
In tumbledown shacks
Down by the river

I. M. Terrell's praiseworthy band embarked on the easily recognizable tune of *Pomp and Circumstance* as the class of 1970 threw their caps into the air, filling the afternoon sky with boisterous cheers, their smiles as bright as the futures that lie ahead of them. From the bleachers either side of the football field, family, friends and well-wishers rose to their feet and added to the racket. Leo Sullivan's baritone shouts drowned out everyone around him – everyone except his older sister Mildred, whose shrill screams were nearly earsplitting.

Leo lost track of his niece in the crowd of graduates that appeared to be one bubbling mass of black gowns and young, jubilant faces, but he spotted her again when Jessica rushed to their side of the field. Leo was grateful the girl hadn't received her actual diploma when she walked across the stage, because the rolled paper was crushed in her dark fist. Her smile was big and toothy. Her mother nearly hurdled a few people in the seats below them as she hurried to greet her.

Leo's eyes glistened as he watched the women embrace. Jessica was an only child, and she was forever the apple of her mother's eye. Mildred squeezed her tightly and rocked side to side. Though he couldn't see her face, Leo knew his sister was crying. His heart swelled with joy as he slowly stepped down the bleachers to join his family.

Afterwards, they celebrated at Mama Ernestine's. There were a lot more hip and teen-friendly eateries in the city, so Leo guessed this wasn't Jessica's first choice. More likely Mildred had selected the restaurant, because it was one of only three black-owned restaurants in the city. In any event, it was an excellent pick. Mama Ernestine's specialized in soul food that would have you thinking your own mother was throwing down in the hot kitchen.

Along with Leo and Mildred, a host of other relatives had come to celebrate Jessica's graduation, a few from as far as San Antonio. In total, there were sixteen members of the family spread out on three long tables. They were lively and ravenous by the time the food was served.

"I'm so proud of you," Grandma Betty called across the table. Her soft voice was barely audible over the sound of silverware clinking on plates that were loaded with meatloaf, mashed potatoes and green beans. "You always make me proud," the matriarch added.

Jessica's smile was adorable as she paused with a forkful of scrumptiousness inches away from her lips. "Thank you, Grandma."

The girl had rich, dark skin, like her mother. She had picked out her afro during the ride from the school, so the indentions from her graduation cap were no longer visible.

"What are you majoring in, when you get to college?" Uncle Jerry asked.

"I'm going to law school," Jessica announced. "Gonna be an attorney, like Uncle Leo!"

That brought a round of *oohs* and approval.

"No, you're gonna be better than me," Leo said. "I can see you moving out of this city and making a difference up north, somewhere like Washington or New York."

At six-three, he was the tallest man at the table. Leo had dark, serious eyes, a full beard shaved low. He kept his hair short, a little bit longer on top. Even without the suit he wore to his niece's graduation, he was a handsome man. But in his professional attire, he was downright dashing.

"I don't think I have to move away to make a difference," Jessica replied to him. "There's a lot of folks around here that need legal help."

"Yeah, and most of them are my clients," Leo joked. "Don't think I'ma allow some little upstart to come take food off my plate!"

Everyone laughed at that.

"What school you going to?" one of the cousins asked.

"Southwest Texas," Jessica said, still beaming.

"That's a great school," Uncle Jerry said.

Leo was surprised to hear a *hmph* from Mildred, who sat next to her daughter. He didn't intend on inquiring about her attitude, but Jerry didn't know any better.

"What's wrong with Southwest Texas?" he asked.

"What's wrong with the *University of Alabama*?" Mildred countered. "That's where she *wanted* to go. I'm not surprised they rejected her, though."

Mildred rocked a natural afro that was a little bigger than her daughter's. Her horn-rimmed glasses made her critical eyes appear even more annoyed.

"Southwest has a good law school," Leo said, hoping to appease her.

"Not as good as *Alabama*," Mildred snapped. "And *you* know that. Of course they doing all they can to keep black folks outta there. Don't know why we even bothered to apply."

"How you know being black had anything to do with them not accepting her?" Uncle Jerry wanted to know.

Mildred gave him a dumb look. "You know we talking about the same school where Governor Wallace had his notorious *Stand in the Schoolhouse Door*, right? There's no way they'd let my baby in after that."

"His stand in the door didn't mean nothing," Jerry recalled. "Kennedy made him let those students in. The national guard showed up, and Governor Wallace got his butt out the way." He chuckled at that.

Mildred dug in her heels. "If you think Mr. *Segregation Forever* – and people who think like him – ain't still running things, you done lost your mind. Jessica graduated with a 3.8 grade point average. Alabama accepted plenty white kids who don't have grades that good. I'm sure it didn't help that Jessica went to an *all-black* high school, but that's another story..."

"You're right," Leo said, eager to stop his siblings' bickering, as he'd been doing since they first learned to talk.

15

"That's another story, and it's not the one we need to be focused on right now. Jessica just graduated. We're supposed to be celebrating – not harping on the negatives. If we spend all our time complaining, we won't never get anything accomplished."

"That's for sure," Jerry agreed.

"And if we *don't* complain, nothing will ever change," Mildred said, always wanting the last word. "But I'ma let it go for now. Today *is* my baby's graduation, and I'm proud of her. She's always been something special. She's gonna keep making us proud."

"Now that's something we can all agree on," Leo said. "Toast!" He raised his glass of iced tea in the air. "To Jessica, may the wind of success always be at your back!"

"Here here!" Jerry said, raising his glass.

"I'll drink to that!" Mildred chipped in.

Her smile was broad now, but Leo knew his sister had more to get off her chest, and he hadn't heard the last of it.

Sure enough, after dinner Mildred tossed the keys to her '64 Ford Falcon to her daughter and told her, "I know you got a graduation party to get to. You go ahead and have a good time. I'll catch a ride home with Leo."

Jessica's eyes lit up. "Really, Mama? I can take your car?"

"Yes, baby," Mildred said, her smile warm and nurturing. "Be safe and try to make it home before the moon gets too high."

Jessica embraced her mother before hurrying to hop behind the wheel of Mildred's most prized possession. Leo waited for his sister to catch up to him in the parking lot.

"Leo, can you give me a ride?"

"Of course I can," he replied, opening the door for her.

When they were both inside the vehicle, her doting expression melted away. "Why do you always have to take Jerry's side?"

"I wasn't taking his side," Leo said with a chuckle. "Just moving things along, so we could get through supper. Seems like you don't have a filter when it comes to bickering. Any time's a good time to speak your mind."

"I didn't see anything wrong with having a friendly conversation about those rednecks in Alabama, but I guess you're right. I certainly didn't want to bring down the mood at my baby's party."

"I know you didn't," Leo said as he rolled out of the parking lot. "And you're right. There's a lot more work needs to be done, as far as those universities. Jessica has every right to go to any school she pleases."

"I'm glad you feel that way," Mildred quipped. "Do you mind heading back to the school for a minute, before you drop me off. There's something I wanna talk to you about."

"What school?"

"The one we just left; the only high school in town black kids can attend."

Leo was perplexed by the request, but he piloted his Cutlass in that direction.

When they neared the downtown area, Mildred stared out of the window at the Trinity River; the largest waterway in the city.

"Remember when all the blacks had to live in shacks in the river bottoms?" she asked.

Leo looked her way and shook his head. "Course I don't remember that, and neither do you. You're talking about back in the 1800s. I know you got an old soul, Mildred. But you not *that* old."

"I didn't have to see it personally to remember it," she replied. "But I read plenty about it. Plus it wasn't that long ago. They didn't start moving us away from there until 1941."

"*Us?* We grew up on the east side," Leo pointed out.

"I mean *us* as a people, knucklehead. You and I were both alive when they had blacks segregated down by the river. Don't you ever take time to look at the bigger picture?"

Leo thought he did so on a regular basis, but apparently he hadn't broadened his horizons enough. "Okay," he conceded. "So they moved us from the river bottoms in 1941. What about it?"

"Up here," Mildred said, as his Oldsmobile climbed a rather steep hill that lead to the school. "Make a right," she instructed.

"We're going to the projects?" Leo asked knowingly.

"Yeah," she confirmed. "For a minute..."

Leo had no idea what he was meant to gain from this excursion, but he continued to drive dutifully. The Butler Housing Project was bustling as the sun began to dip in the western skies. It didn't take much observation to realize the residents were all black and all living at or below the poverty line. Skinny children clothed in hand-me-downs made the best of their existence, playing chase or stick ball. Some entertained themselves with a worn basketball on one of the courts that had been erected.

The adults loitered about aimlessly, as far as Leo could tell. Young men in their late teens and early twenties spied his car suspiciously, possibly wondering if he'd come to score drugs, or maybe he was someone they could prey upon. Many of the young women lounged complacently on their porches; tending to the next generation who were still in diapers.

"Henry H. Butler's probably rolling in his grave, seeing what happened to his namesake," Mildred said as Leo followed the loop that would lead them back to the school.

"Henry Butler?"

She sighed, fixing disappointed eyes on her brother. "Leo, Overbrook Meadows hasn't had too many black leaders. The least you could do is remember them. They named these projects after Henry H. because he was so prominent in the 1800s. He always looked out for his people."

"Sorry. I didn't know this was gonna be a history lesson."

"It's not just history," Mildred argued. "It's *right now*. It's 1970, and we still got all these black families segregated from the rest of the city; living just as poor as they did when their grandparents were down by the river."

"But they could move," Leo argued, "if they chose to. There are plenty of black families living elsewhere in the city."

"Sure, they could move," Mildred said, "but with what money? What job? And what education? And that brings us back to this, this *horrible* place," she said as Leo rounded the corner and I.M. Terrell was once again in view.

Contrary to his sister's disdain, Leo always thought the high school was beautiful, especially now, in the waning sunlight. He'd graduated from Terrell in '53; in the same football field that hosted Jessica's ceremony. It might have been nostalgia, but he had fond memories of his high school days.

"I'm sure you know who Isaiah Milligan Terrell was," Mildred said as he pulled to a stop in front of the school.

"Of course," Leo replied. "I think knowing who he was is still a requirement for every student enrolled here."

"How do you think he would feel about this being the only black high school in Overbrook Meadows – *still* – in 1970? The Supreme Court ruled on Brown versus the Board of Education in 1954, but Overbrook Meadows still has segregated schools. How the hell is that possible, Leo?"

He had no idea. "I suppose they just haven't gotten around to it..."

Mildred's frown told him how inadequate that response was. "You know parents have to bring their kids from as far away as Arlington, Burleson, Benbrook, *Weatherford* – because they don't have any black high schools at all. This is the *only* one. Do you know how many white high schools they have to pass on the way here? It's ridiculous, Leo. So many of our leaders died so we wouldn't have things like this, not still around in *1970*.

"I have great memories of my time at this school, just like you do. I believe our teachers gave us the best education they could, considering we didn't have many facilities, and all of our text books were old; handed down from the white schools. But now, *today*, the fact that this school is still open

20

is a testament to how much we've yet to accomplish. This building is a *monument* to racism, Leo, and I need you to do something about it – those projects too."

His eyes widened. "*Me*?"

"Yes, you! Why not you? We don't have a Henry H. Butler or I.M. Terrell around anymore, but we got you. You're a prominent figure in the community, just like those men were."

"I – I have to disagree with you there. I haven't accomplished a fraction of what those men did. I'm not a community leader, Mildred. I'm just a lawyer, not even a civil rights lawyer."

"You're the most prominent black attorney in this city – yes or no?"

"I, I mean..."

"You know damn well you are. People look up to you, Leo. They come to you when they have a problem; whether it be with the police, their landlord, *whoever*. And you always look out for the people. You even help them when they can't afford it. I know you've never been an activist, but you know right from wrong, and you can see this school and those projects are 100 percent *wrong*."

"Wha, what am I supposed to do about the projects? You want them shut down too? Where would all the people go?"

"I don't have a solution for the projects," Mildred acknowledged. "But this segregated school is in violation of the *law*, and you're a lawyer, so I know you can do something about it, if you put your mind to it."

Leo couldn't deny the school was illegal, but he doubted he could do anything about it. Surely others had already tried and failed. He knew he'd never get Mildred out of his car if he told her that, so he nodded, looked her in the eyes and said, "I'll look into it, see what I can do."

She stared back at him for a few beats before nodding as well. "Okay, Leo. I'ma hold you to that. Don't think I'ma let this go."

"No," he said, sighing inwardly. "I'm sure you won't."

CHAPTER TWO
MAYOR HOLLOWAY

O Captain! My Captain! Shut down this wretched school!
Certainly separate, never equal. The Supreme Court has
ruled!
These black chilluns deserve better; better books, supplies
and such
We pay taxes for white schools. Why should they have so
much?
Obey the law! Do what's right!
Stop playing us for fools!
You got all the power, Mayor
Shut down this wretched school!

On Monday, Leo arrived at his place of business at
8:30 a.m. Located at the intersection of Main Street and
Northside Drive, he never failed to appreciate how fortunate
he was to have the coveted space. Only ten minutes from
downtown, his office was in view of businessmen and women
commuting from work as well as cowboy enthusiasts, who
traveled to the historic district to explore the rustic
environment that had been preserved.

Once inside, he was greeted by his receptionist/paralegal/personal assistant Ruby, who never complained about the many hats Leo asked her to wear.

"Good morning, Mr. Sullivan!"

She smiled as she stood and crossed the room, headed to a fresh pot of coffee she had brewing. Ruby wore a white blouse with a pencil skirt that accentuated her thin frame. She was attractive, but in the six years she'd been employed, Leo never made the mistake a lot of men in his position did. Despite how much time they spent alone, cooped up in the small office, he valued Ruby's expertise, not her looks.

"Good morning," he replied. Before continuing to his office, he asked her, "How was your weekend?"

"It was great," she called over her shoulder as she prepared his drink. "My sister and her husband came from Waxahachie. I don't get to see my nieces and nephew that often. Took 'em to the community center and had a pool party."

"Really? I didn't get an invite," Leo teased.

"That's because I knew you were busy with your family. It was your niece's graduation, right?" She turned and handed him a steaming cup with one spoonful of sugar and a dash of cream; just the way he liked it.

"Yeah," Leo confirmed. He transferred his briefcase to his left hand and accepted the mug.

"How was it?"

"It was great. What's not to like about a graduation?"

"Where'd y'all go afterwards?"

"Ah..." Leo's eyes became dreamy. "Mama Ernestine's."

"Ooh, I know that was good!" Ruby exclaimed.

"Always is. We all left that place as full as ticks."

"What about your niece? What are her plans for the fall?"

"Southwest Texas," Leo informed her. "Her mom was dead set on Alabama, but the powers that be decided otherwise – which reminds me; can you get me some information about I.M. Terrell?"

"Sure. What do you need to know?"

"Why it's still open," Leo said. "All public schools are supposed to be integrated. It's 1970, and we still have segregated schools."

"Hmmm. Is this for a case you're working on?"

"Lord, I hope not," Leo said honestly. "I was talking to my sister on Saturday–"

"Say no more," Ruby said with a chuckle. "If this is Miss *Angela Davis'* new cause, I know she won't give you any peace until you get to the bottom of it."

Leo grinned. "You know her so well. Let me know what you find out," he said before ducking into his office.

"Sure thing."

Leo was fully immersed in a few cases he'd been working on when his secretary stepped into his office a couple of hours later. Ruby carried a stack of papers and wore a look of confusion.

"Busy?"

Leo was, but he looked up from his desktop and gave her his full attention. "No, what's up?"

"I looked into that I.M. Terrell situation, and…" She shrugged. "I can't find a reason why our schools are still segregated. It seems like this city is taking its sweet ol' time getting caught up with the north."

Leo sighed. "That's what I was afraid of."

Ruby sat across from him and placed the papers on his desk. "I'm sure you know the Brown versus Board of Education suit struck down segregated schools in 1954, but many cities are dragging their feet on implementing it, sometimes being outright defiant."

Leo nodded.

"I'd say our city's history of segregation is… *interesting*," Ruby continued. "Even before the passage of the Civil Rights Act in '64, the Leonard Brothers, who own the biggest department stores downtown, took down their "Colored" and "White Only" signs. Everyone else followed suit. By 1963, all of our department stores were fully integrated, which led to the decline of our black business district, but that's another story.

"As far as the schools," she said, "we actually have several integrated elementary schools. It's anyone's guess why they haven't gotten around to the middle and high schools, but we certainly have the law on our side. The Civil Rights Act reaffirmed all public schools should be integrated. In 1968 the Supreme Court once again ordered all states to dismantle segregated schools '*root and branch.*'

"Initially they said states should integrate schools with 'all deliberate speed,' but mayors were using that clause to take their time. In 1969, the Supreme Court declared that was insufficient. Another ruling ordered the '*immediate*' desegregation of schools.

"I'd say addressing the city council would be the best way to get to the bottom of this – but we only have two friendly faces there. Dr. Edward Guinn is still there. You know he was the first black elected political figure – in '67. Last year we picked up another black councilman named Mario Pratt."

Leo's eyes widened. "We didn't have any blacks elected to office until three years ago?"

"Overbrook Meadows' history with racism may not seem as bad as other cities," Ruby informed him. "We didn't have any Emmett Tills or marches, like in Birmingham. But we also haven't made much progress. Far as I can tell, the blacks here never really stirred the pot. I don't want to say we've been complacent, but I can't find many instances where we rocked the boat; tried to disturb the status quo."

Leo suddenly felt guilty for the way he'd responded to his sister yesterday. Was he part of the problem? If he wasn't part of the solution, he certainly was – according to Mildred, at least.

"Thank you," he told his secretary. "You've done a great job."

"Sorry I couldn't get the answers you needed," she replied.

"No, you've got plenty," he said, looking over her reports. "The black city councilmen, you wouldn't happen to have their numbers, would you?"

"Right on top," Ruby said.

Leo studied her paperwork more closely and saw the phone numbers jotted down. "You're always on the ball." He gave her a pleasant smile as she rose to her feet and returned to her desk.

Councilman Guinn wasn't in the office, but Mario Pratt answered after a few rings. Leo introduced himself, and the man seemed to recognize his name.

"Mr. Sullivan! How are you? How's business?"

"The business of suing is always booming," Leo declared.

Mario laughed. "Yeah, I bet it is! I hope you're not calling about any lawsuits coming *my* way."

Leo found that comment odd but didn't take the time to process it. "No, not at all. I'm actually calling about a civil rights issue."

"Civil rights?"

"Yeah. My niece graduated from I.M. Terrell this weekend, and my sister's upset that she had to attend a segregated school. All the research I've done indicates we should have fully integrated schools by now. Was wondering if you could tell me what the hold-up is."

"You were hoping *I* could tell you?"

"Well, sure," Leo said. "You're on the city council."

"Barely," Mario argued. "I was elected last year. Haven't been here long enough to make the kind of changes you're asking about."

"You think integrating our schools is too much to ask for?"

"No, I'm not saying that. The way change is coming, I'm sure it won't be long."

"But you haven't asked about it at your meetings?"

"No, Mr. Sullivan. It's not something that's come up. We've been dealing with the budget; the firemen's pension has been taking up a lot of our time."

"Well, *can* you bring it up?" Leo wondered. "How long would it take before you could get some answers?"

After a pause, Mario asked, "Are you, is this related to a lawsuit?"

Leo had no intention of suing anyone, but he liked that the possibility seemed to worry Mr. Pratt.

"I have a potential client who wants answers," he said vaguely.

"Well, why don't you call the mayor?" Mr. Pratt suggested. "If he wanted our schools integrated, he could have it done by the time school starts in the fall."

Leo didn't like how this supposed *voice of the people* was playing dodge ball with what he considered a basic question, but he let him off the hook.

"What you're saying is the mayor is the reason we still have integrated schools, even though the Supreme Court has ruled against it several times over..."

"Yessir. The buck stops with Woodrow Holloway."

With an annoyed sigh, Leo said, "How about you give me Mayor Holloway's number, save me the trouble of looking it up."

Mario quickly rattled off the digits.

Leo placed his second call and was greeted by a Caucasian woman.

"Mayor's office."

"Hi. I'm attorney Leo Sullivan. May I speak to the mayor, please?"

"What's this regarding?"

"I'd like to know why we still have integrated schools in Overbrook Meadows," he said boldly.

After a pause, the woman said, "One moment."

Leo wasn't sure what type of response he expected, but he did *not* expect her to return to the line a minute later and tell him, "Mayor Holloway can meet you this afternoon at one-thirty."

Leo was so surprised, he almost said *Really?* Instead he told her, "That's great. I'll be there."

After lunch, he headed downtown and found a parking spot in front of City Hall. He had a few minutes to spare, so he looked over the reports Ruby had given him, while rocking his head to The Moment's latest hit, *Love on a Two-Way Street*.

He left his car at a quarter after one and entered the local government building with butterflies in his gut. As a lawyer, he'd always felt comfortable about his preparation and delivery. But politics was foreign territory for him. To make matters worse, he was taking his complaint all the way to the top.

In the mayor's office, he was greeted by a middle-aged redhead, presumably the woman he'd spoken to earlier. After identifying himself, he was asked to take a seat directly across from her, while she picked up the phone and announced his arrival. When she hung up, she looked him in the eyes and said, "He's ready to see you. It's the door at the end of the hall."

Leo stood and said, "Thank you," before heading in the direction she'd given. He developed tunnel vision as he walked down the hallway. The door straight ahead of him was the only one open. As he drew nearer, he saw the mayor's office was brightly lit, with large windows that offered a magnificent view of downtown.

Leo stepped inside and found the head honcho sitting behind a Cherrywood desk that was free of clutter. The office, on a whole, was large and neat. In the back corners stood two six-foot ficus trees with leaves so perfect they had to be artificial. The room smelled of stale cigarettes, though Leo didn't see an ashtray on the mayor's desk. His eyes returned to the center of attention as Woodrow Holloway rose from his executive chair.

The mayor stood a few inches shorter than Leo and thirty pounds heavier. He was cleanshaven with short, blonde hair, a pudgy nose with reddish cheeks. He wore a white, collar shirt with no tie. His sportscoat was draped over the back of his chair. It wasn't very warm in the room, but the man's forehead glistened with a thin coat of sweat. Leo found his palm equally moist when he reached to shake his hand.

"Good afternoon, Mayor. I'm Leo Sullivan."

The white man nodded, rather than return the greeting. He took a seat with a grunt and invited Leo to do the same.

"Have a seat, Mr. Sullivan."

Leo did so.

The men took a few moments to size each other up before the mayor asked him, "To what do I owe the pleasure of this meeting?"

Leo was sure his secretary had told him why he was there, but he didn't mind going through the formalities.

"I'm here to discuss the problem we seem to be having with school integration."

The mayor's eyes narrowed before he responded. "I wasn't aware we had a problem. Who says we do?"

His southern twang was rich and easily identifiable as Texan. Leo knew the mayor had lived in Overbrook Meadows all his life and was the product of a good-old-boy network of firemen, politicians and law enforcement. His father had rose through the ranks in the police force and served as the chief for ten years before retiring. His grandfather led the city's first fire department, but most of the blacks in the city knew him best for being photographed at a lynching.

Leo took all of this into consideration as he looked him in the eyes and said, "You don't think it's a problem that we still have an all-black high school and plenty of white schools that won't allow Negroes to enroll?"

After a pause, the mayor said, "It's not something I'm proud of, but it's also not something I'd consider a *problem*. I'm sure the schools will be fully integrated in due time."

Leo frowned. "*In due time*? That's a rather vague statement. Care to be more specific?"

"Who's asking?"

Leo looked around the office before his eyes returned to the man in charge. "Well, seems like I am."

The mayor's cheeks became a darker shade of red. Leo recognized malice in his eyes before the sweaty man sighed and calmed himself.

"I understand you're the one asking the questions at this moment, Mr. Sullivan. What I'm asking is who sent you? Are you working on some sort of lawsuit?"

This was the second time someone assumed his interest in integration meant there was legal trouble brewing. Again, Leo decided to run with it.

"I haven't been paid a retainer, so technically I wouldn't say the interested parties are my clients. But I expect a check any day now..."

"And who might those parties be?"

"I'm sure all of the pertinent information will be included in the paperwork I file at the courthouse," Leo replied.

Mayor Holloway shook his head slowly. "Mr. Sullivan, I think the school board is handling the integration issue as fairly and expeditiously as possible, given the current climate. They've already integrated a few grade schools. I believe they're going to work on one of the middle schools in the fall. If your *interested parties* would exercise a little patience, this matter will resolve itself in due time."

"You keep mentioning this *due time*," Leo noticed. "But I think the time for all of the schools in Overbrook Meadows to be fully integrated is *now*. Integrating one middle school in the fall only means all of the high schools will remain segregated for at least another year. Frankly, we find that unacceptable."

"I think it'd be wise to look at the bigger picture," the mayor replied. "You want the schools integrated, but at what cost? I know you don't want riots, people protesting at the school doors. You've seen what this type of agitation leads to in other cities in the south. The good people of Overbrook Meadows are *almost* ready to take that final step, but not quite. If we don't take our time and do this carefully, the outcome could very well be *dangerous*."

Leo didn't have to look down at his notes to tell him, "The Supreme Court ruled in 1958, *Cooper versus Aaron*, that the fear of social unrest or violence, whether real or constructed by those wishing to oppose integration, does not excuse state or city governments from complying with Brown versus Board of Education."

The mayor sucked air between his teeth before fixing a hard glare on his visitor. "It's easy for men in fancy robes to make decisions from far away in *Washington* – a lot harder to get southern cities to implement those decisions. I told you we're working on integrating the schools, and I suggest you give us time to do our job. Certain folks would not like to know you're over here stirring up trouble about something that's basically a non-issue. If I were you, I'd tread lightly, Mr. Sullivan."

Leo wondered who those certain folks were. Folks like the mayor's grandpappy? He hoped Mr. Holloway couldn't tell his mouth had gone completely dry when he asked him, "Is that a threat?"

"Of course not," the red-cheeked man said, his features softening. "Good day to you, sir."

Leo remained seated for a second, stunned the meeting had ended so abruptly and rudely. The mayor continued to stare him down until Leo rose to his feet.

"Good day to you too," he said before exiting the office.

CHAPTER THREE
EBENEZER BAPTIST CHURCH

Fire burning in our bellies
Target sighted
Munitions ready
Precious Freedom is the prize
The scope trained on naysayers
Hold it steady
I reckon they ready for a fight
They see us coming
Not one of them running
They're holding it down for southern pride
But they lost that fight in 1865
They've got the money
They've got the power
David versus Goliath
But we don't cower
Every movement
Starts with one move
And a bold leader
Will it be you?

Leo was rattled when he left the mayor's office, but he felt irritated and energized by the time he returned to his sanctuary. He was eager to tell Ruby how his visit went. When he was done talking, she wore the same look of disbelief Leo must've worn when he sat across from the mayor.

"He threatened you?"

"I asked him if it was a threat," Leo reported. "He denied it was. Either way, it's not enough to file a complaint."

"But still," Ruby said. "That's serious."

Leo nodded. "Yeah, it is."

"Are you worried?"

"Worried that he'll, what, have me gunned down in the middle of the street?"

Ruby shook her head. "No. Nothing that drastic. But people might start harassing you, if you push this."

"I'm not worried about harassment."

His secretary raised an eyebrow, which made Leo chuckle.

"Okay, I know I'm not a martyr," he said. "To be honest, I don't think I've ever stood up for anything important. But I'm not afraid to stand up for this."

"What if it starts to cost you business?"

Leo hadn't considered that, but he held fast. "Anyone who wouldn't hire me because I want to get our schools integrated – I don't need their business."

Ruby watched him for a few beats before nodding. "Okay."

"What about you?" he said. "You worried about getting involved?"

"No, not me. I've got far less to lose than you. What's the plan? What can I do to help?"

Leo rubbed the sparse beard on his chin. "By the end of the week, the mayor will know I haven't filed a lawsuit," he surmised. "He'll think my visit was the end of it, but I'm ready to crank up the pressure. I know me and Mildred aren't the only ones upset about I.M. Terrell. We need to come together; see how many likeminded folks are willing to stand with us."

Ruby continued to nod. "That's a good idea."

"Can you make some calls?" he asked. "I'd like to have a meeting. I'll call my sister, to see how many people she's already talked to."

"Okay," Ruby replied dutifully. "When would you like to have the meeting?"

"Sometime this week, if possible. Thanks ahead of time," he said, before heading to his office. "I appreciate your help."

"Hey, it ain't charity," Ruby joked. "Long as I'm getting paid, I'll call whoever you want!"

Ruby worked on nothing but his request for the next few hours. By the end of the day, her calls had yielded fruit. She came to his office a few minutes before closing time and sat across from him.

"You were right," she said, looking down at her notes. "There's a lot more people interested in shutting down I.M.

Terrell, besides you and your sister. I'll make more calls tomorrow, but so far I've got more than a dozen people who've agreed to attend your meeting. A few of them are white, too."

"That's great," Leo said, his eyes widening. "Have you picked a date – and location? I think this office is a little too small for that size crowd."

"Oh, it definitely is," Ruby agreed. "How's Ebenezer Baptist Church sound to ya?"

Leo grinned. "It sounds great – and plenty big!"

"I talked to Pastor Warren," Ruby reported. "He's all for the meeting and wants to have it after service on Sunday. He offered us the cafeteria, which can seat over a hundred people."

Ebenezer Baptist was not only the largest black church in the community, but it was a historical landmark. Standing tall on Berry Hill, the property was once a plantation. Childless, the slave owner left the land to his widow. And upon her death, in an act of kindness Mother Teresa would be proud of, she left the property to a family of former slaves, who still resided there as sharecroppers.

Miraculously, the Warren family managed to hold onto the land for over a hundred years. They sold a dozen acres here and there, mostly to get through the Great Depression, but the bulk of it remained black-owned and virtually untouched by modern and industrial development. Pastor Jeremiah Warren lived there in a beautiful ranch house with his family. Fifty yards away, his magnificent church stood at the top of the hill.

"You're one of a kind," Leo told his secretary. "Have I told you lately how blessed I am to have you here?"

"You have," she admitted. "But it never hurts to hear it again."

On Sunday, Leo arrived at the church early enough to attend the morning service, which he thoroughly enjoyed. If he was ever inclined to attend church on a regular basis, Ebenezer would be a great place to call home. But for now, he would much rather sleep late on Sunday mornings. It was God's day of rest, after all.

After Pastor Warren concluded his sermon, collected his offering, and the choir sang one last spiritual, the congregation was dismissed. Leo hoped they'd all stick around for his meeting, but he wasn't bold enough to try to corral them. If the pastor wanted them to attend, he would've made a special announcement. But a good number of them did stay. Leo was surprised by the number of people who hung back, looking in his direction for guidance.

He in turn approached the pastor, who finally made a formal announcement.

"Everyone who's here to meet with Mr. Sullivan regarding the integration issue can make your way to the cafeteria. It's right down this hallway," he said, approaching a door to the left of the altar. "I'm sorry," he told Leo, as the crowd began to head in that direction. "I meant to make an announcement during the service."

"No, that's fine," Leo said, reaching to shake his hand. "I appreciate you for allowing us to meet here."

The pastor had dark skin with a cluster of moles on both sides of his face. His hair and goatee were salt and peppery, mostly salt. He was a tall man with a booming voice that was also soft and compassionate when he needed it to be.

"Think nothing of it," he said. "The church is always here for the community, especially in times like this. I wish you the best of luck, son."

Leo remained in the sanctuary a while longer, greeting and directing new arrivals to the cafeteria, before he headed that way himself. When he stepped through the double doors, he was shocked to find more than forty people inside. He was certain all of them hadn't come in from the worship area. He spotted another entrance near the back of the cafeteria and guessed some had skipped the sermon and come directly from outside.

That was fine with him. Leo wore a warm smile as he quickly made his rounds, greeting some of the faces he hadn't seen before. In addition to his sister and a handful of her friends, Ruby was there as well as Mario Pratt, from the city council. The rest of the crowd was strangers, mostly women. Only one of the attendees was white, rather than the "few" Ruby had mentioned. But Leo was glad to have her.

His spirits were high as he returned to the front of the room and told everyone, "Why don't you all take your seats, so we can get started. I don't wanna keep you too long."

He waited a few seconds for them to follow his instructions. Soon dozens of expectant eyes were focused keenly on him. Leo couldn't deny the sense of pride and responsibility he felt at that moment. He was glad they were at a church, because he needed the Lord to guide his words and his steps, if he was meant to guide them.

"Thank you all for coming," he said. "I didn't expect this big a turnout. I hope you're all here to figure out what we can do to get our schools integrated. 'Cause if you're waiting on a bingo game, you might have picked the wrong day."

They laughed politely at his joke.

"No, but seriously," Leo said. "We do have a serious problem on our hands. Last week my niece graduated from I.M. Terrell, and I'm sure you know that's an all-black school. In fact, it's the only high school in Overbrook Meadows black students can attend. And while I'm not knocking the education our children receive there – I graduated from the school myself, and many graduates have gone on to achieve greatness – that doesn't excuse the fact that black students have separate and *unequal* facilities.

"The Supreme Court ruled against segregated schools over fifteen years ago. I know it takes time for the court's decisions to get fully implemented, and some cities have faced fierce opposition to integration. Sometimes the opposition comes from as high as the governor. But that should not excuse us from doing the right thing.

"So, what I'd like to do today is brainstorm; see what ideas some of you have." When no one spoke up right away, Leo added, "This is an informal discussion. Feel free to speak your mind."

"We need to sue!" someone near the middle of the room suggested.

The comment was met with approval from the crowd.

"That is an option," Leo said. "The only problem is lawsuits take time. It could easily get bogged down in the courts. If we're talking about a civil rights lawsuit, it could take years before we get a settlement. I was hoping we could

41

get this settled in the next couple of months, so our children can attend any school they want in the fall."

The crowd mulled that over, and a woman asked, "What about the school board? Has anyone spoken to them?" The woman was attractive, rocking a natural, curly 'fro.

Leo was momentarily distracted by her looks, but he recovered quickly. "That's a great idea. I talked to the mayor earlier this week, and—"

"Holloway's a damn racist!" one of the few male voices in the room shouted.

Leo didn't like the idea of someone swearing in the church – or the church's cafeteria – but he didn't mention it. "Yeah, I'm sure you're right about that," he replied. He told them about his brief encounter with Mayor Holloway.

"He threatened you?" Mildred asked from a seat at the front of the room. "Leo, why didn't you tell me?"

"Because there was nothing I could do about it," he said. "Even if it was a more concrete threat, the mayor is over the police department, so who would I run to?"

That brought grumbles of resentment; the kind that served to unify an oppressed nation.

"I think we need to start with the city council," another woman said. "If we could at least get the issue up for a vote, that would be a first step."

Most people agreed with that, but one person voiced her dissent. It was the same woman who had caught Leo's attention a moment ago.

"If we had effective leaders on the city council, this would've been taken care of years ago."

Leo forced himself to keep his expression neutral, though he was taken aback by her daring. There was a member of the city council in the room with them. Mario Pratt wasn't sitting too far away from the brooding princess.

"It's a lot easier said than done," the councilman said in his defense. Mario was a thin man with fair skin and straight hair; courtesy of an acid permanent. "I can get *some* things accomplished in City Hall," he continued, "but you have to remember there are only two black faces there. Even if we got integration on the ballot, we'd be outvoted. It's like I told you on the phone," he said to Leo directly, "anything that happens in this city is ultimately up to the *mayor*. If he wants the schools integrated by fall, you'd better believe he'd get it done."

"Well, how do we pressure him to do it?" Leo asked, eager for solutions, rather than excuses.

"That's the million-dollar question," Mario said.

Leo frowned and looked away from him. "Okay, who else has an idea?"

"If the mayor is the problem, then maybe we need to get him outta there!" a fiery brother suggested. "We ain't never gon' get nothing accomplished, if we got a racist running the whole city."

A good number of people in the crowd voiced their agreement.

"Alright," Leo said nodding. "But I don't know anything about politics. What does it take to get a mayor to step down? Doesn't he have to commit some sort of offense?"

"He's not gonna step down," Mario said knowingly. "Holloway loves being the fat cat. But, you know there's an election coming in a couple of months. This may be a longshot, but it might be possible to get him *voted* out of office."

Leo raised an eyebrow as excited murmurs spread through the crowd. "Okay." He nodded. "But what are the odds of that? And who's running against him? It wouldn't do any good if the next mayor is just as bad."

"That's why I said it's a longshot," Mario stated. "He only has two challengers, and neither of them is expected to get over ten percent of the vote."

The excited murmurs became disappointed grumbles.

"What if we throw our voice behind one of the opponents?" Leo asked, not wanting to let the idea go. "Maybe they're not favored to win now, but if we've got two months to sway the vote, we may be able to change the outcome."

"That might be doable," Mario acknowledged. "But who's to say backing them would do anything about integration? I don't know either of the candidates very well, but far as I can tell, they're cut from the same cloth as Holloway. I don't think you wanna put a lot of time and money behind another racist."

"That wouldn't make any sense," Mildred agreed.

"What we need to do is get us a mayor who we *know* will integrate those schools," someone suggested. "That's the only way to be sure!"

Everyone in the cafeteria agreed with that suggestion. Leo's eyes returned to the only politician among them, but he already had an idea what Mario would say.

"Don't look at me!" the councilman blurted. "My plate's too full. As a matter of fact, I was thinking about stepping down from being a councilman next year."

"But you're the only—"

"*You* should run!" Mildred said, cutting her brother off.

Leo's eyes widened. "Wha – *me*?"

"Yeah, that's a great idea!" the other outspoken man in the room said.

Leo's mouth fell open when he looked around and saw the smiles blossoming throughout the room.

"Oh no, no, no, no, no..." he said, shaking his head. "There's no way."

"Why not?" someone wanted to know.

"I don't know how many times I have to say this, but I'm not a politician," Leo repeated.

"That's not a disqualifier," Mario stated. "The mayoral race is mostly a popularity contest. The south is filled with mayors who've never held office, up north too."

"But you just said Holloway had the race in the bag," Leo argued. "If those other candidates don't stand a chance against him, surely I'd stand even less of a chance."

"Not if you run on the integration platform," the beauty with the serious eyes said. "That would get a lot of people on your side right off the bat. Plus you're plenty popular. You're the best lawyer in town, white or black. And you've already got a reputation for standing up for the little guy. Everyone knows you look out for the community. You underestimate yourself."

Leo wasn't sure what a *platform* was, but there were a couple of things he did know: He liked the way the woman sang his praises, and her encouragement lit a fire in his belly. It was almost enough to make him go along with this preposterous plan – but he caught himself.

"I don't have time to run for mayor," he told the crowd. "Definitely don't have time to *be* the mayor, if I actually win. I'm so busy with my law office, I don't make it out of there till sunset some nights."

"Sometimes you gotta make sacrifices for the greater good," Mildred chided him. "Do it for the children, Leo. You know what's important, otherwise you wouldn't have called us here today."

The guests certainly agreed with that. They were getting more riled up by the second.

"Plus the mayor's not that busy," Mario chipped in. "I assure you, you'll be able to keep your law office up and running. In a small city like this, being the mayor is more like a part-time gig."

"You're killing me man," Leo said in exasperation. "You know *you're* the best choice for this."

More grumbles from the crowd made it clear none of them favored Mario for the task.

"Nah, man," the outspoken brother in the room said. "It should be you, Mr. Sullivan!" To Leo's surprise, the man stood and rocked his fist in the air. "*Leee-oh! Leee-oh! Leee-oh!*"

It didn't take long before the whole room was caught up in the hysteria.

"*Leee-oh! Leee-oh! Leee-oh!*"

Leo palmed his face and finally gave in. But there were still the practicalities to consider.

He lowered his hand and said, "Okay, okay. Let's say I did run for mayor–"

"*Yay!*" they cheered.

"Wait, wait... Let's say I did *try* to run for mayor," Leo continued, "you know I have absolutely no idea how to go about it."

"Maybe my campaign manager can help you," Mario said right away. "She got me on the city council, and I didn't have any idea what I was doing either."

Of course Mario had another easy answer. Of course he did.

"Who's your campaign manager?" Leo asked with a sigh.

"Carla Hunter," the councilman said. "Much as you been talking to her this afternoon, y'all should make acquaintances."

Leo was taken aback. "I've been talking to her?"

The woman with the beautiful eyes and curly afro stood, and Leo took in her full physique for the first time. Slender, yet curvy. Brown skin like his. She wore a loose-fitting blouse with a long skirt that was appropriate for church or the office.

"I'm Carla Hunter, and it would be my pleasure to help you run."

Leo could do no more than stare and blink at her while the rest of the group rose to their feet, promising him votes and donations, time and energy, even blood, sweat and tears, if need be.

CHAPTER FOUR
CARLA

After the meeting, Leo hung around and accepted more congratulations and promises of support from the attendees. He appreciated every one of them, but he knew it would take a lot more than the forty supporters, if he was to stand a chance against Holloway. In his peripheral, he noticed Carla hanging back as well. He didn't make eye contact with her, but he kept up with her as she moved about the crowd. Soon it was just the two of them in the cafeteria. Leo knew that *she* knew he'd want to discuss her duties, should he take her own as his campaign manager.

But not to be presumptuous, he approached her and said, "I would like to talk to you about what Mario said; about you helping with my campaign. Do you have time?"

"Sure," she replied. Her lips were full, her eyes serious again.

"I don't know about you," Leo said, "but I'm long overdue for lunch. You hungry?"

She nodded. "Yeah. I was thinking the same thing."

"Okay. Let me go find the pastor and thank him for letting us use his church. I'll meet you in the parking lot."

Finding the pastor was no easy task. The older man had already retreated to his home and had settled down for his own lunch.

"Don't mention it," he told Leo over a plate of fried porkchops. "Care to join us? You hungry?"

Checking out the spread the pastor's wife had put together, Leo considered asking Carla if she wanted to stay there and dine with them. But with the pastor, his wife and their four children, the dining room was too crowded for the meeting he wanted to have with Carla. He preferred a quieter, cozier atmosphere.

"Looks great, but no thank you," he replied. "Did Ruby discuss using your cafeteria again next weekend?"

"No, but you're welcome to it, for as long as you need."

"I'm glad you said that," Leo told him, "because they've got a wild idea that I should run for mayor. Our Sunday meetings here might turn into my political headquarters, if I decide to go through with it."

The pastor chuckled pleasantly. "I'll be cold and dead in my grave, before this town elects a black mayor."

"*Jeremiah*!" his wife admonished him. "Don't you be saying nothing like that at the supper table, 'specially not in front of the kids."

The older children smiled at that. The youngest one giggled.

"Sorry," the pastor said. "It's 1970, and a black man can be whatever he wants. Who knows? We might even have us a black *president* one day." He could barely contain his sarcasm. "Feel free to use the cafeteria for as long as you like, Mr. Sullivan. That's what this church is here for; to serve the community."

When he got to the parking lot, Leo was disappointed to see that Carla hadn't waited for him. His chest warmed when he spotted her waving at him from the driver's seat of a '59 Sierra wagon.

He approached her car and said, "Sorry I took so long."

A cursory scan of her vehicle revealed it was in decent shape, with no car seat for an infant or any other items that might indicate she was a wife or mother. There was no ring on her left hand, so this made sense. But why would a single woman need such a big car?

"It's no problem," she said. "Where are we going? I could follow you or meet you there."

"Henry's shake joint on Riverside is pretty good, if you're up for burgers."

She nodded. "Okay. I'll see you there."

Leo didn't like the idea of her waiting for him a second time, but he told her, "Alright, I'm right behind you," before she rolled out of the parking lot.

Henry's didn't have the best hamburgers in the city, but their fries and shakes were incomparable. Leo and Carla found a booth near the front window. They sipped their shakes while waiting on the main course. Leo had already noticed how beautiful she was, but sitting so close, he thought he'd met her before their encounter at the church.

"I swear I've seen you somewhere before," he said, knitting his eyebrows.

"Maybe," she replied. "I've seen you at a couple of events, most recently at your niece's graduation last week."

Leo's eyes brightened. "You were at Terrell's graduation?"

She nodded and wrapped her lips around her straw. Leo watched the sweet vanilla slide up to her mouth.

"I apologize for not remembering," he said.

"It's okay. I don't expect people to remember me, but you're sorta famous, so I recognized you."

"I don't know why you keep saying that. I'm not famous."

"You don't have to be modest," she replied. "We don't have many successful black men in Overbrook Meadows. Everyone knows them by name and sight – well, the blacks certainly do."

"Okay." Leo nodded. "Were you at the graduation supporting family?"

She shook her head. "No, I was there for the students. I'm at all of the graduations – and every school day too." She smirked at his puzzled expression. "I'm a teacher," she revealed. "I teach government at I.M. Terrell."

"Oh, wow. That's a noble profession, but, um... It's interesting that you would come to a meeting that's strategizing to shut your school down. Are you sure that's what you want?"

"Oh yes, I'm very sure. I've been teaching for twelve years. The one thing I've always wanted is to give the kids the best education possible, the best facilities, the best chance of making a difference in this world. We can put them on the right path at Terrell, but everyone knows they deserve better. They deserve better adding machines, better books, smaller classrooms.

"Everything we have comes from the white schools – after they upgrade to the newer version. Our classrooms are so packed, we don't have time to give the gifted students the individual attention they deserve, unless they can stay after school, but that's not always possible, especially with some of them coming all the way from Weatherford.

"I'm not worried about finding another job, when they finally close Terrell's doors. We'll still have the same number of students in this city, they'll just be spread out more. There will be a need for someone to teach them."

Leo nodded. "That's true. It's awesome to meet someone who's so vested in the next generation."

"The students are my life," Carla explained. "I've always done everything I can for them. Me and a dozen more teachers, we wake up early to pick up as many as we can, from some of the outlying cites. If not for us, a good number of students would have to go without a formal education."

That explained her station wagon. Her dedication made Leo's heart swell. "You call me a community leader," he said as the waitress delivered their burgers. "But it seems like you and your colleagues are accomplishing a lot more than I am. I'm humbled by your efforts."

"We all do our part," Carla said, reaching for a French fry. "We have to. Can't expect anyone else to help us."

They were quiet for a few minutes as they dug into their meals. After a while, Leo brought up something that had been on his mind since the meeting.

"It seems like everyone is against the idea of Mario running for mayor…"

Carla's features immediately filled with disdain. "We're better off with Holloway. At least with him, we know what we're getting. A snake like Mario, he'll support whatever cause is paying him the most. That Negro is the definition of a *corrupt politician.*"

Leo chuckled. "Let him tell it, you're the one responsible for getting him elected."

"One of my biggest regrets. We finally get a couple of our people on the city council, and one of them cares more about his pockets than the color of his skin. I'm surprised he came to the meeting. Can't trust that man no further than I can throw him. Wouldn't be surprised if he was spying on us."

Leo shook his head, grinning. "So, what you're telling me is, you don't care for Mr. Pratt," he joked.

"Yes, that's what I'm telling you," she replied, cracking a smile. "So much time and energy wasted. He wouldn't have made it anywhere near the city council, if it wasn't for me."

This was the first time Leo heard her take credit for her hard work.

"What qualifications do you have to be a campaign manager?" he wondered.

He thought he asked the question innocently, but he noticed her blush, despite her skin tone. She shook her head.

"I don't have any qualifications to be a campaign manager, his or yours, except from what I know about city government from my teaching job. I learned a lot more while working on Mario's campaign. But to be clear,

53

'Campaign Manager' is not something I could list on my resume."

"Now I think you're the one being modest," Leo said. "If you did it before, I'm sure you can do it again. How many people do you have to get elected before you can list it on your resume."

She noticed him smiling, and she smiled too.

"I guess if I can help get you elected, that would solidify it."

"I agree. So, tell me how we'd go about it."

"Well, to simplify, you should try to get some experience first..."

"Really? *Now* you say this, after I tried to tell everyone at the meeting how unqualified I was?"

She giggled. Her expression was usually serious. Her amusement warmed Leo's insides.

"There's more than one way to gain experience," she explained. "You could get involved in community activities, which I believe you already do with your legal work. You should build relationships with local businesses. Again, I think you've already got that covered."

Leo nodded. He couldn't deny that he had.

"Ideally you should run for a lower office. *But,*" she said, before he could protest, "we already agreed that's not a prerequisite. You need to start attending city council meetings. You need to create a committee that will be your campaign team. I think everyone at the church agreed to participate in that. You'll have to fill out some forms downtown and start a petition to formally run for mayor. You'll need signatures. I'll check to see how many."

Leo blinked quickly, trying to keep up with her. She said she wasn't a campaign manager by trade, but he couldn't tell. He grew more impressed with her by the second.

"Once you get all of your paperwork submitted, you'll officially be on the ballot. After that, you have to campaign. You already have your platform."

"Integration," he said.

"Right. *Vote for Leo to End Segregated Schools*."

"That doesn't even sound like a lofty ambition, hearing you say it."

"It's not. It's very serious, and very important."

"Yes, of course you're right."

"While you're running for mayor, you'll need lots of donations," she continued. "The campaign trail is very expensive. You'll have to advertise and meet with a lot of businesses and organizations. You'll have to do a lot of public speaking. I know that's not something you'll shy away from."

"And what are you basing that on?"

"Your meeting today," she said, "the way you carried yourself. You come off as very approachable and determined. You know how to hold an audience's attention."

"I sounded determined at the church?"

"You did until they talked you into running," she said with a smirk.

"To be honest, this all sounds like a mountain of work."

"It is. That's why you have your campaign team behind you. And that's why you have me."

He knew what she meant by that statement, but he couldn't stop his mind from hearing it differently.

That's why you have me.

Leo couldn't remember the last time he was this taken by someone he'd just met.

"Do you really think I can win?" he asked.

"It's an uphill battle," she conceded. "Mario's right about the support Holloway has. He's heavily favored to win another term. Plus you're black, and this isn't exactly New York City. Heck, I don't even think New York is ready for a black mayor. And you've only got two months to campaign.

"The only reason I'd say you've got any shot at pulling this off is your platform. It will sway a lot of white voters. Recent polls have found that 65% of Americans believe schools should be integrated."

"I think I heard about that poll," Leo said, his eyes narrowing. "Didn't they break it down, though, with the opinion of northerners versus southerners?"

Carla looked away for a moment, as if she'd been caught cheating. "Yes," she admitted. "Seventy-six percent of northerners are in favor of integration, but only thirty-three percent of southerners feel the same way. But we're gonna win this thing," she said, her eyes bright again.

Leo nodded and smiled politely. It was clear he was not convinced.

CHAPTER FIVE
MOMENTUM

Miss Hunter be teaching
She be rocking that 'fro
When she write on the blackboard
Her hips sway to and fro
When she walk up to my desk
And get personal
One-on-one
She be giving some wisdom
And I be listening, but some-
Thing about her smile
Got me wishing that she
Was much younger
Or I was older
Cause if I was, maybe we
Could ride off in the sunset
Ain't got no car, but I can dream
This ain't nothing but a crush
Only thing on Miss Hunter's mind
Is teaching

Word of Leo's new ambitions quickly spread throughout the small town, and things heated up quickly. The following Sunday, even more volunteers showed up to throw their support behind the new candidate. True to her word, Carla began to play a major role in the meetings, as this was her area of expertise.

That afternoon, she brought the necessary forms for Leo to officially declare his candidacy. Everyone in the church's cafeteria gathered around, some looking over his shoulder, when he signed them. When he inked his John Hancock on the final page, the crowd erupted in cheers, as if he'd signed the Civil Rights Act.

As an attorney, Leo was accustomed to being the center of attention in the courtroom, but this type of adoration was humbling. He was grateful when Carla resumed her role as the leader of the meeting.

"Okay, folks. I'll get these papers filed on Monday, but getting Leo on the ballot is just the first step."

Today she wore a floral print dress that didn't accentuate her figure, but her sleeveless arms were enough to catch Leo's attention. Her skin was smooth, her hands delicate. Her demeanor was friendly yet focused.

"The next step is to gather 5,000 signatures to announce his candidacy," she said. She toted a file folder stuffed with papers. She gave a stapled bundle to every attendee as she made her way through the cafeteria. "I know that sounds like a lot, but there are almost 50 people here today. If each one of you gets a hundred signatures, that's all we need."

Smiles were abundant as the crew accepted their task and their papers.

"We'll get the signatures," Mildred assured her.

"Do we have to get white people to sign?" someone else asked.

"No," Carla responded. "It doesn't matter if all of these signatures come from black people. But we will need white votes to get Leo elected, so we might as well start getting them onboard."

Leo watched her from a seated position at the front of the room. He imagined this was how she went about her usual duties as a classroom teacher. He grinned, thinking of the crush he would've developed if he'd been one of Miss Hunter's students when he attended I.M. Terrell.

When she was done passing out the papers, Carla said, "Another thing we need to start working on is fundraising. This will probably be one of the most challenging duties, because many of us are from poor communities. According to the latest statistics, nearly 70 percent of the blacks in Overbrook Meadows are currently at or below the poverty line."

Leo was stunned by that number. He knew there weren't a lot of black professionals in the city, but he had no idea their condition was so bleak.

"You can start raising funds while gathering the signatures," Carla went on. "Most people will say they can't afford it, but encourage them to give anything they can; a dollar, fifty cents, whatever. You'd be surprised by how quickly it will add up. In the meantime, Leo and I will go after the bigger donors; the business owners and wealthy citizens. But that's not to say you can't go after them as well. We all have to do everything we can to make this happen."

The attendees nodded, still energized, despite the enormous mission that lie before them.

"Before you leave today," Carla said, "I would like to get started on the fundraising." She crossed the room to where her purse sat on an empty table. She fished for her wallet and produced a ten-dollar bill. "It's okay if you can't give this much," she said. "Seriously, anything you can offer is fine. If you don't have anything right now, please try to bring something next Sunday. And... I think that's all we have for today."

Leo's heart thumped uncomfortably. Ten dollars was a good chunk of change. It was enough to feed a family of four at one of the nicer diners downtown. He hated to see her part ways with the bill for a cause he still deemed unrealistic.

Carla met his gaze.

"Is there anything else?" she asked.

Leo shook his head. "I don't have anything. To be honest, you're leading this group a lot better than I could have. You've only been my campaign manager for one day, and I can already admit I'd be lost without you."

There was no change in the hue of her dark, brown skin, but Leo was almost positive he'd made her blush. He stood and removed his wallet from his pocket as he approached her. He didn't count the bills inside, but he knew the largest was a twenty and there were several singles. He gave all of it to Carla.

"I hope this helps."

She watched his eyes as she accepted it. "Thank you, Leo. This will go a long way."

He backed away as the others came forward to offer what they could. Carla's enthusiasm grew with each bill she added to the stack. Leo knew this was all for him, but he was more pleased that Carla was happy.

On Monday, he wasn't surprised when his campaign manager showed up at his law office bright and early. With school out for the summer, Carla had little to do, aside from getting him elected.

After greeting him and Ruby, she followed Leo into his office.

"Do you have a busy schedule?" she asked. "I'm gonna start calling some of the local businesses, but it's helpful if they hear from the candidate himself. I was hoping you could do some fundraising of your own, starting with some of your clients."

She stood before his desk dressed professionally in a white blouse and black skirt. She toted a black briefcase that was well-worn. Her other hand gripped a small paper bag, which presumably contained her lunch.

"Ruby and I haven't gone over my agenda for the day," Leo replied, "but I'm sure I can make time to call a few people."

Carla nodded. "Great." She looked around his small office before asking, "Do you have somewhere for me to work?"

As much as Leo would've liked to have her within eyesight all day, they both needed their space.

"I have a third office," he replied, "but I use it for storage. I can clear the desk off for you, if you don't mind working around a bunch of boxes filled with court papers."

"No, I don't mind. And I can clear the desk myself. Just point me in the right direction."

"It's the first office on the left, when you step out of here," Leo said, his eyes curious. "Are you sure you don't want me to straighten it up for you? I don't go in there very often. There's liable to be a few spider webs."

"I think I can handle it," Carla assured him.

Leo's eyes rolled down to the swell of her backside when she turned and walked away from his desk. He couldn't help himself.

"You won't see me jumping up on a chair over some spider," she commented.

He chuckled. "No, Miss Hunter. You don't strike me as that type."

Ten minutes later the sounds of manual labor in his storage room finally stopped, and he heard Carla make her first call. Ruby stepped into his office at the same moment.

"Your campaign manger, she's not one to request or accept much assistance," she noticed.

"No," Leo said with a smile. "She's not. It took a good deal of willpower to remain planted in this seat while she worked in there. Were you able to see what she was doing?"

"She cleared off that desk," Ruby reported. "She asked me for a box to put the files in and asked if I needed them sorted any kind of way. But she wouldn't let me help her – said she didn't want to pull me away from what I was doing. I felt guilty, because I wasn't doing too much. But that one – she's pretty strong-minded."

"I've noticed," Leo replied. "It sounds like she's done now, starting to make her calls."

"Sounds like it," Ruby confirmed. "Should I expect her to be around on a daily basis?"

"I'm not sure. I'll ask her before she leaves. Do I have a lot going on today? She wants me to make some calls; do some fundraising on my own."

"Your schedule's not too packed, but I can move a couple of things around, to make sure you have time to make those calls. I don't think Miss Carla is the type of woman you'd want to disappoint."

Leo grinned at that. "Yeah, I was thinking the same."

Carla worked till two p.m. on Monday. She didn't tell Leo how much she'd secured in donations, which he took to mean she hadn't done very well. But on her way out, she was optimistic.

"Not a lot of money raised, but I'm certainly getting the word out. A lot of people are excited to hear you're running. I didn't realize Holloway had so many dissenters out there. Any luck with your calls?"

Leo was embarrassed to shake his head. "No, but I did get a few promises to vote for me. I guess that counts for something."

"It certainly does!" Carla said. "Don't worry. The donations will pick up. Times are hard. No one wants to feel like they're throwing money down a well. Once people start to take you seriously, they'll be more eager to put their hard-earned dollar on the line."

"Yeah, about that... To be honest, I feel guilty about the funds we're raising. We're accepting money from people who really can't afford to give. I mean, I'm a longshot anyway, right? You don't really think I have a chance, do you?"

Carla gave him a look that made him feel lower than a horned toad.

There was no humor in her eyes when she said, "Maybe *that's* why you didn't raise any money today. If you don't have confidence in yourself, you shouldn't expect anyone else to. Are you ready to throw in the towel already? If so, you need to let me know, because I usually work a part time job at JC Penney's during the summer. If Terrell's still gonna be open in the fall, I'm passing up money I need to spend on school supplies."

Leo was taken aback. "Uh, no. I'm not saying that. I just..."

She propped a hand on her hip while she waited for him to finish his sentence.

"With you running things, I believe anything's possible," he decided. "I'll be sure to exude more, um, *confidence* when I make calls tomorrow."

"That would be great," his campaign manager said, though it didn't look like she believed him. "You have a nice evening, Leo."

On her way out of the office, he heard her tell his secretary the same. Ruby appeared in his doorway thirty seconds later. She leaned on the doorframe and stared at her boss, grinning like the Cheshire Cat.

"Hmph. I guess she told you."

"Yeah, she did," Leo admitted, and then his eyes widened. "Wait, are you sure she's gone?" The thought of Carla catching them discussing her spooked him more than it should have.

Ruby laughed at that. "My, my..." she said before returning to her desk.

Leo frowned but didn't respond to that.

CHAPTER SIX
STICK TO LAWYERING

To smile at her
And see her smile back at me
To see the twinkle in her eyes
When I've done something pleasing
Is all I want these days
She's my heart
She's the reason
For the sun and the moon
Every star
Every season exists for her
She's a goddess
I'm a minion
I understand I'm not worthy
But ever so often the queen
Scans her queendom
And spots me
Ah, those eyes…
How I live for her smile!

The rest of the week proceeded similarly, with varying degrees of success. Carla arrived bright and early each morning and found herself staying later and later. She made so many calls in her cozy, little office, Leo thought she might be reaching out to the whole directory.

Each day she brought her lunch in a brown paper bag. Leo learned the bag always contained the same items; a bologna sandwich (sometimes with cheese), an apple and a granola bar for dessert. Rather than pop, she drank from the water cooler in the office. Leo offered to take her to lunch on Tuesday, partly to thank her for her hard work, but mostly to lure her into a dating-type atmosphere, but she turned him down.

She smiled politely and told him, "I already have a lunch, thank you. But if you'd like to put the money you planned on spending on my meal towards your campaign, that'd be great."

Tuesday was also the day Leo secured his first donation all by himself. After the reprimand he received from Carla on Monday, he dared not give her the same report on day two. He phoned a couple of his black clients; both of whom had heard he was running for mayor but had no funds to offer at the time. On a whim, he called Ronald Mooney next. Ronald owned a profitable auto salvage business. He'd been very appreciative a few months ago when Leo represented him in a land dispute that added nearly twenty acres to the junkyard.

Ronald had not heard of Leo's new goals.

"Heh, heh. Mayor of what?"

"Of Overbrook Meadows."

"Yeah, right."

"I'm quite serious."

"Holloway's the mayor."

"Yes, but it's not a life-long term," Leo informed him. "He's coming up for reelection in a couple of months, and I'm gonna run against him."

"Heh, heh. Yeah, right."

Leo subdued his frustration and said, "I don't know if you're laughing because you don't think I can make it, or you don't think a black man can be mayor. But either way, you're wrong."

"Hold on, now. You know I ain't got nothing against blacks. I hired you for my lawyer, didn't I?"

"Yes, you did. I won that case, and your salvage yard got a heck of a lot bigger because of it."

"I paid you your fees," Ronald said, sensing a trap.

"I'm not calling for more money," Leo said. "Well, technically I am, but not for the work I did for you. I would like to know if you'd be willing to donate to my campaign. Running for mayor is hard work, and it's expensive. I really could use your support."

The man on the other end of the line sighed. "Why the hell are you running for mayor? I like you, Leo. You're a decent fellow, in my book. But you know there ain't a chance in hell of you beating Holloway."

"I'm running to put an end to segregated schools. I.M. Terrell is the only high school available for black students, and it's illegal, and it's a shame. I talked to Holloway about doing what's right, and he's dragging his feet. Seems like the only way to get things done is to do it ourselves, so I'm running for mayor."

"And you want me to help you? I don't think some of my customers would be too happy about me supporting your cause, Leo. Just being honest."

"You could donate anonymously," the lawyer offered. "No one would ever know..."

After another long exhalation, the white man said, "I'll give ya fifty dollars."

Leo's eyes lit up. "I'll take it!"

He rushed to Carla's office a moment later.

"I just got a fifty-dollar donation!"

In his excitement, he didn't realize she was on the phone, until she held a finger up and continued her conversation.

"Thank you very much, Mrs. Woods. We really appreciate your support. I'll send someone to pick up the check tomorrow morning."

She hung up and gave him her undivided attention. "You got fifty dollars?"

Her smile was genuine, but Leo suddenly felt foolish for disturbing her with the announcement.

"Oh, well, yeah. But, I mean, it's no big deal. I'm sorry for interrupting your call. I'll, um, I'll let you get back to work."

He started to back out of the office, but she said, "Wait."

He paused in the doorway.

She told him, "Fifty dollars is a lot of money! I'm proud of you! I knew you could do it!"

Leo felt this was the same kind of encouragement she'd give one of her struggling students when they exceeded expectations. His smile was sheepish when he responded.

"Thank you. I'm, um, I gotta get back to work now."

"Way to go, Leo!" she called as he disappeared from sight.

Leo made eye contact with his secretary as he passed her desk. Ruby rolled her eyes and brought a hand up to cover her grin.

"Don't you say anything," Leo mumbled and continued to his desk.

On Sunday, there were more new faces in the crowd of likeminded individuals who had come to fight against segregation. Leo's heart swelled when he entered the church's cafeteria and saw nearly 70 people waiting for his leadership. There were even a couple of white faces seated before him. Leo thanked them for their support and then called Carla to stand by his side, because it was *her* leadership that had gotten them this far.

"Thank all of you for coming," she said, easily taking control of the meeting. "I see a lot of new faces out there, which is great! We're gonna need all the help we can get. I believe I've spoken with all of you directly, but if not, please don't leave today before giving me your name and number. At our last meeting, Leo signed the petition to formally run for mayor, and those papers have been filed and accepted by City Hall!"

She paused while everyone cheered that declaration. She half-turned and looked Leo in the eyes as she joined the adulation.

"Last Sunday we also passed out papers," she continued, when the applause died down, "so everyone could start collecting the signatures needed to announce Leo's candidacy. I've spoken with most of you during the week and collected your signatures, and at last count, I believe we had thirty-five hundred of the five thousand we need. Is that right?" she asked Leo's sister.

Mildred sat at a table with a pile of papers neatly stacked. "That's right," she said with a smile. "A little more than that."

"For those of you who haven't turned your signatures in yet," Carla said, "please give them to Mildred at this time, so we can find out if we hit that magic number."

Leo watched his campaign manager appreciatively as the crowd began to stir. He didn't realize Carla had been speaking with the team throughout the week, and he didn't know she'd begun to delegate responsibilities. He didn't even know the number of signatures they'd collected. Each time he thought his level of admiration had peaked, Carla exceeded his expectations yet again.

"While Mildred's counting the new signatures," she said, quieting the group again, "We need to talk about our next step. Leo's integration platform should be enough to get the votes we need to win, but the message doesn't mean anything unless we get the word out. Next Sunday we'll start to work on *visibility*. We're gonna need campaign posters, flyers, signs on shop windows and telephone poles. We need to blanket the city; so you can't go more than ten blocks without seeing Leo's name on something.

"At our next meeting, I want all of you to pitch in. We need poster boards, stakes, paint, paintbrushes, crayons, whatever you have. We need you to talk to people in your neighborhood, to see which neighbors and businesses will be okay with a sign out front. We have to come up with some catchy slogans. '***Leo for Mayor***' isn't enough. Our signs need to mention our platform, which is school integration.

"And it would be great if you could bring your children to our next meeting. Everything we're doing is for them, so they should be involved. They could draw on the posters or make some themselves. When people see posters drawn by the kids, not only will they be eye-catching, but it'll drive the point home.

"So why don't we separate into groups for a while and see what slogans we can come up with. Marci, could you make rounds with the groups and jot down the best ones. We'll get the list narrowed down to the top three by next Sunday."

"Okay!" a woman who was a stranger to Leo said, and then the attendees began to gather in small groups as instructed.

Leo's mouth hung open when he turned to Carla.

"You already know everyone by name?"

"Not all of them," she said. "Marci teaches with me at Terrell. And of course you know your sister."

Leo thought her smirk was adorable.

"This is amazing," he said. "*You're* amazing."

"I'm just doing what I can to help," Carla responded. "You're the reason everyone's here. We wouldn't even have a campaign, if not for you."

By then Leo was used to her deflecting praise, but he was not used to *her*. Even with all of the time she'd spent in his office, he still considered her a mystery.

Twenty minutes into the brainstorming session, Mildred caused the group to erupt into cheers again.

"***Five thousand***!" she shouted, looking up from her stack of signatures. "We got five thousand signatures, and we still have all these to go!" she said, pointing to another sizable pile of papers.

"*Yay! We did it!*" someone shouted, and then the campaign team broke into a chant the man of the hour didn't think he'd ever get used to.

"**LEO! LEO! LEO!**"

Pastor Warren popped in at that moment and smiled broadly as he took in the scene. When they quieted down, he said, "I would love to see this kind of enthusiasm for the word of God next Sunday! I know most of you only came for the meeting, but don't forget we actually have church here too!"

They laughed good-naturedly, but Leo could tell the pastor was serious.

After the meeting, he hung back and accepted more praise from his team. Carla stayed too. She collected the names and numbers for the newcomers and doled out more responsibilities to the ones she'd come to rely on.

When it was just the two of them in the cafeteria, Leo approached her and asked, "Are you in a rush? Got time for lunch?"

"I could eat," she replied. "Where do you want me to meet you?"

They met at Papa Lou's Barbecue restaurant on West Berry for what had to be the most succulent rib sandwiches in the south.

"Where are you from?" Leo asked as they got started on their meal.

"White Settlement."

He grinned at that. The town was a northwest suburb of Overbrook Meadows.

"Is it true the city was named that because of all the white people who live there?"

"It is," Carla replied.

Leo raised an eyebrow. "Really?"

She grinned. "Yeah, really. Back in the day, there were two settlements in the area. One was almost 100 percent white, and the other was occupied by Native Americans. The white folks didn't want visitors to get confused about which town they were going to, so they named theirs *White Settlement*."

"Wow. That's one of the most racist things I've ever heard. After all these years, no one ever wanted to change it; the name of the city?"

Carla grinned. "You're asking if white people want to undo something that shines bright as a reminder of their superiority? Yeah, right. That's like asking if they'll take down the thousands of confederate monuments scattered throughout the south."

Leo shook his head. "So, you left, to get away from the blatant racism?"

"No, I left because there was nowhere for me to be a high school teacher in my hometown. Terrell's the only black high school for more than thirty miles in either direction. Haven't you been paying attention?"

"I have," he said. "And don't worry, I'm taking this just as seriously as you."

"I know you are."

"But, I must say, you're outworking me at every turn. There's no way I could've put this campaign together without your help. The way you've brought everyone together–"

"No, it's *you* who brought everyone together. You don't hear them chanting my name, do you?"

"I'm just the figurehead," Leo argued. "I may be the face of the movement, but you're the backbone. You're the brains behind everything."

"The same could be said about Martin Luther King. He showed up and gave the speeches and led the marches, but there were many, many people putting the dates and times and paperwork together; collecting money, getting the word out to let folks know King was coming to town."

"Don't compare me to Reverend King."

"Why?" she asked. "You don't think you're worthy?"

"You know I'm not."

She looked him in the eyes, hers were unblinking. "I know you can achieve a lot more than you think you can. If you believed in yourself half as much as the people at the church do, you could make a change Leo. You could change the whole world, just like Reverend King."

Leo's heart stuttered. He didn't know if she truly believed that, or if this was another motivation tactic. But the look in her eyes invigorated him. With a woman like her by his side, there was no limit to how much he could accomplish.

He caught himself before the words in his heart floated out of his mouth.

"Are you enjoying your lunch?" he asked instead.

She smiled brightly. "You better believe it. This sure beats my bologna sandwiches!"

Leo laughed. "Yeah, I bet it does!"

They were in good spirits when they exited the restaurant thirty minutes later. The good times came to an end as they neared the parking lot. A '56 Desoto with the convertible roof peeled back came to a stop next to the curb when the driver spotted Leo and his campaign manager. There were three more good old boys inside the vehicle. The bright afternoon sun shone brightly on their pale skin.

The driver said something to the passenger who wiped the sweaty hair from his brow as he eyed Leo. Sensing danger, Leo subconsciously took a step forward and to the left, effectively shielding Carla from whatever trouble these men might seek to cause.

"Hey, ain't you that Sullivan fella, what work at that office on Main Street?" the passenger asked.

He was a redhead, with a distracting gap between his teeth. His smile was sadistic. Leo noticed all of the men in the car had similar grins. They appeared to be in their early to mid-twenties.

Leo's body was tense, his expression set in a frown when he responded.

"Who wants to know?"

"*Who wants to know?*" one of the men in the backseat mocked.

The one sitting next to him laughed.

The driver leaned forward, so he could see past his passenger, and said, "You best stick to lawyering!"

"And that pretty, young thing you're with should stick to *teaching!*" the passenger added.

The smiles never left their faces. In fact, the men laughed as the driver pulled away from the curb and rejoined the lazy, Sunday traffic. One of them, Leo couldn't tell which, shouted, "*White schools for whites!*" as they drove away. "*Nigger schools for niggers!*"

Leo's face flushed with heat. His eyebrows bunched together in rage. But his expression softened when he turned to check on Carla. She didn't look upset, rather her eyes were as determined as ever.

"They seem to know a lot about us," Leo grunted.

She shook her head slightly. "They know you're a lawyer, and I'm a teacher. That's not a lot. That's basic information."

"I'd still like to follow you home," he said, "to make sure you don't have any trouble when you leave here."

Given her strength and overall feisty nature, he thought she'd scoff at the idea.

But she surprised him by saying, "Okay, Leo, if it'll make you feel better."

CHAPTER SEVEN
AUDACIOUS

Carla lived in a modest two-bedroom home in an east side neighborhood known as Meadowbrook. They didn't spot any suspicious persons or vehicles in the area when they pulled into her driveway, but Leo exited his car and asked to accompany her inside.

"I don't think that's necessary," she replied. She looked up and down her quiet street, checking to see if any of her neighbors were out.

"How do you know someone didn't break in?" Leo asked. He offered a hand to help her out of her car. "They could be in there now, waiting on you." He eyed the house suspiciously.

Carla gave him a look as she rose to her feet. "If that's your way of making me feel safe, I'd say you're doing it wrong."

"Sorry. I do want you to feel safe. That's why you should let me follow you in – and stay for a while. Just in case."

"Hmph. Yeah, right. Can you imagine what my neighbors would think if they saw you?"

"It's broad daylight."

"Plenty illicit things happen in broad daylight, Mr. Sullivan."

"I'm more concerned about your safety than your reputation."

"I can take care of myself," she replied. "Been doing just fine all these years."

"How many carloads of white men have threatened you *in all these years*?"

She sighed. "I see you're not gonna let this go..."

He shook his head.

"Well," she said, stepping past him, "come on then."

Her home was exceptionally neat. Leo wasn't sure why, but he expected a teacher's house to be filled with clutter; piles of worksheets and ungraded papers on every surface, balls of paper tossed towards the trashcans but not inside.

Instead he encountered hardwood floors that were swept clean and waxed. Her living room was sparsely furnished with a sofa, loveseat, coffee table and floor model television. There were a few portraits of what he assumed were her family hanging on the walls.

He told her, "Nice place."

"Thank you." She crossed the room gracefully.

Her skirt was knee-length and form-fitting. She wasn't overtly curvaceous, but Leo found it hard to take his eyes off the swell of her hips and backside. She paused in the hallway and looked back at him.

"Do you want to check the rooms yourself, or do you trust me to do it? I'm not sure if I left any of my unmentionables lying around."

Leo felt she was patronizing him, but the thought of coming across her underwear made his mouth go dry. "Go ahead," he said, taking a seat on the sofa. "If you see something, or *someone*, just give a holler. I'll come running."

"Got it," she said and continued down the hallway. "Unless they sneak up from behind and throw a hand over my mouth," she called from an unseen position.

"You won't think it's so funny if that really happens," Leo said. She didn't respond to that. After a full minute, he still hadn't heard from her. "Hey, you okay?"

He heard her footsteps before she reappeared in the hallway. Rather than pumps, she wore flip-flops now. Leo saw that she'd removed her stockings to make space for the shoes to slide between her toes. He was taken aback by both the sight of her bare feet and bare legs. The latter were shaved smooth.

He recovered quickly enough to look her in her eyes and respond when she said, "Yes, I'm fine, Leo. Sorry to keep you waiting."

"It's no problem."

"Are you ready to leave, now that you know I'm safe?"

He shook his head vacantly. "Those guys might be on their way here now. I think I should stay, a little while longer."

If she suspected his reason for wanting to be in her presence might be a bit nefarious, she didn't mention it.

"Fine. Would you like some coffee? I think I have some cheesecake too."

A smile spread across Leo's face. "Sure. I'd like both."

Ten minutes later, they sat at the kitchen table with their coffee and dessert. Leo noticed this room was as quaint and neat as the front room. The only thing out of place were a few clean dishes on the drying rack, but he could hardly fault her for that. The cheesecake was as succulent as the company. As he sipped his coffee, his thoughts kept returning to her bare legs and feet below the tabletop. He wished she'd brought the treats to the living room, so he could steal a few more glances while they ate.

"I still can't believe they threatened us," he commented.

She asked him, "Why do you find it so hard to believe?"

"We're not even close to integrating those schools."

"That just means they're taking us seriously. They already view us as a threat. You didn't expect everyone to roll over and let it happen, did you?"

"No. I guess not. But threatening a lady, a school teacher..."

She smirked at that. "This is the same country that killed Viola Liuzzo, just five years ago."

Leo had heard about that. To his recollection, she was the only white woman ever murdered while fighting for black people's civil rights.

"And Reverend Klunder," Carla said. "If they'll run over a white preacher in broad daylight, you know they have no problem threatening little, old me."

"Klunder?" Leo was puzzled. "Never heard of him."

"That's by design," Carla said. "One of the most powerful tools of white supremacists is the control of information. It won't be long before they start saying the civil war had nothing to do with slavery." She shook her head and chuckled, and then her expression became serious. "Reverend Klunder was one of a thousand people protesting a segregated school being built in Cleveland, Ohio. The school board figured if their *current schools* had to be integrated, they could build a brand-new school and make sure it was only for whites."

Leo frowned. "But that doesn't make any sense."

"Of course it doesn't. By law, the new school would have to be integrated too. But they weren't thinking that far ahead."

"And Reverend Klunder, you said he was a white man?"

She nodded. "The protesters started marching on the worksite, making it hard for the construction workers to get anything accomplished. There was a bulldozer... A few protesters stood in front of it, and some stood behind it; hoping the driver would give up. The guy that was driving, he *says* he didn't know Reverend Klunder was behind him. The police bought his story. No charges were ever filed."

"He ran over him?"

"Completely." She shook her head. "Flat as a pancake."

Leo grimaced. "Well, did they stop building the school, at least?"

She sneered. "Nope. They finished building that school."

His eyes widened. "No."

"They did, Leo. It's standing tall right this moment."

"How long ago did this happen?"

"Six years. Not that long."

He could do no more than shake his head.

"Just because we've never had a Medgar Evers or Reverend Klunder, doesn't mean Overbrook Meadows isn't as racist as Selma or Montgomery. The problem is the white establishment has never really been challenged here. You know we didn't get our first Negro on the city council until three years ago. And the *Overbrook Meadows Telegram* didn't hire its first black reporter until *this* year."

"*This year?*" Leo couldn't believe the city's largest newspaper had gone so long without a black reporter.

"His name is Cecil Johnson," Carla informed him. "He's a great writer. I would love to meet him one day."

"I'm so blind," Leo said, rubbing his face. "I've been living in my own little bubble, thinking we're making progress."

"We are, Leo. We're making progress all across the country. But your campaign is challenging Overbrook Meadows' white establishment. You're running for *mayor*, for Christ's sake. It don't get no bolder than that. So, yeah, expect some resistance. I'm sure we'll get more than a few idle threats, by the time it's all said and done..."

An hour later, they were back in the front room. Sunset was an hour away, and Carla's eyelids were starting to droop as she lounged on the loveseat with one leg tucked beneath her. Leo wondered if she would've taken an afternoon nap after church, if it wasn't for his intrusion. He wouldn't mind fully reclining himself. He wondered what Carla's bedroom looked like. He imagined himself lying with her, spooning blissfully.

"I should leave," he stated, but he didn't rise to his feet. "I wish there was a way I could know you're safe tonight."

"You could call me," she offered. "Only death would keep me from taking your call."

He rolled his eyes at her dry humor. "After what you told me about that preacher in Cleveland, I don't see how you're able to joke about this."

"I don't think one car full of rednecks would qualify as a bona fide death threat."

"Why are you not married?" he asked. "If there was a man here to protect you..."

Her look of offense made him swallow the rest of his sentence.

"Oh, so I need a *man* to protect me? The shotgun leaning against my bedpost ain't good enough?"

"Well, um, I'm sure it is. I just mean, you know, in general, why haven't you married?" he backtracked.

Her eyes were fierce when she told him, "I don't know. Maybe there's not a man out there who wants a woman who thinks for herself; who has her own mind and opinions that are just as valid as his."

"Fancy yourself a feminist?"

"No. I don't mind cooking and cleaning, doing the laundry. But if I work late one night, I don't wanna come home to some man demanding his dinner; trying to shoo me off to the kitchen. As a matter of fact, if he gets home before me, and he knows I'm working late and I'm tired, he should have a hot meal ready for *me*."

Leo grinned at her audacity, but she wasn't done.

"But me working late shouldn't be a prerequisite to him cooking. I want a man who wouldn't mind cooking for me sometimes *just because*. And he could rub my feet as much as I rub his."

Leo chuckled. She assumed he was mocking her unrealistic goals.

"So, you can see why I've never married," she said. "Most men think I'm too strongminded. I guess they're probably right."

"I don't think you're too strongminded. I've just never heard a woman speak like that before."

"And it amuses you?"

"No," he said. "It intrigues me." His eyes left hers, swam down her frame, devoured her exposed leg and settled on her barefoot and perfect toes. When his gaze returned to hers, he said, "If I was your man, I wouldn't mind rubbing your feet *every night*. I don't care if you had a hard day or if you ever rubbed mine. I wouldn't mind one bit."

She sucked air between her teeth. Leo saw the muscles in her neck grow tense. Flustered, she had to lower her eyes.

She told him, "I – I think it's time for you to leave."

Leo grinned as he rose to his feet. His face and chest were warm. For the first time since he'd met her, he felt like he had the upper hand. He wasn't sure how to harness this newfound energy, but he savored the feel of it.

"Will I see you tomorrow?" he asked before turning and heading for the door.

"Yes. I'll be at your office as usual. The battle has only just begun."

She sounded like she'd regained her composure. Sure enough, when he looked back, her eyes were once again focused on his.

"Yes, it's only just begun," he agreed. He wondered if she knew he was referring to his advances as well as their fight for the mayor's office. His smile deepened as he exited her home.

CHAPTER EIGHT
CITY COUNCIL

The next morning Carla made it to the office at 8 am, as was her custom. She actually beat Leo there. She was already making calls when he showed up at 8:30. Leo stopped to greet his secretary before his campaign manager called him into her office.

"Leo, got a minute?"

"Sure do." He left his briefcase at Ruby's desk and stepped into the adjacent room with his cup of coffee. "Good morning."

The dress Carla wore that day was unflattering, but it didn't take much to bring out her beauty. Her slender neck and smooth arms made Leo long to see more of her dark skin. Her curly afro was as majestic as a lion's mane.

"Thought you might want an update," she said, looking up at him. "With that call, we just secured over $6,000 in donations!"

Leo's mouth fell open. *"Six thousand dollars?"*

"Yeah," she said, smiling brightly. "Six thousand!"

"Wha, but, but *how*?" he wondered. "From *who*?"

She laughed. "From all over, Leo. From nearby businesses. Out-of-town businesses. Even some from out of state. Everyone at the church has been helping too. You know Pastor Warren has been taking a separate offering just for you. Everyone wants you to make it. They want the schools integrated by the fall."

"That, that's amazing. *You're* amazing."

"It's not just me. Your whole team has been working hard, getting the word out. Speaking of which, do you think we can clear out these boxes and bring in some tables and chairs, some more phone lines? I wanna bring in more people to help me; turn this into a war room."

"A war room?"

"Like at the church, only smaller."

Leo nodded. "Okay. I can have that done by this afternoon."

"I talked to Ruby this morning," Carla said. "She said you're free at one, so I was thinking we could go down to City Hall. They have a city council meeting today. You need to start attending as many of those as possible."

"Okay..."

"You've got a little buzz," she continued, "but it's not enough to get the votes you'll need to upend Holloway. You need to be way more visible. I need you out there shaking hands, kissing babies. You haven't done any public speeches. We need a *ton* of those. It doesn't have to be anything formal. It doesn't matter if you're at a grocery store or standing on a street corner. If people stop to hear what you have to say, take advantage. The longer you talk, the more people will stop to listen."

"Okay..."

She cocked her head. "Are you with me, Leo? You seem a little lost."

"No, I'm just – I'm blown away by how much you're doing. Every day I'm more awed by you."

"That's great, Leo. But snap out of it. We got too much to do, for you to be standing over there all dreamy-eyed."

He smiled at that. This was the Carla he was used to. It was nothing like the woman who suggested he leave her home yesterday, after he offered to rub her feet. He wondered if he'd ever get a chance to knock her off kilter again.

"Alright," he said. "I'm fine, and you're not that amazing."

"Yeah, right," she said and returned her attention to the papers on her desk. "Talk to you in a few."

An hour later, Leo and Ruby were in his office; discussing a case he'd been neglecting, when Carla rushed in.

"*Guess what!*"

Leo was surprised to see her so animated. "What?"

Carla took in the scene and realized she might be interrupting. "Oh, I'm sorry. Were you guys busy?"

"No," Leo said, before his secretary could contradict him. "What's going on?"

"I got you an interview!" Carla gushed, her eyes wide again.

"Really? That's awesome!"

"Guess who's interviewing you..."

Leo shook his head, grinning. He had no idea.

"*Cecil Johnson!*"

"Wait, *the* Cecil Johnson, the guy you were telling me about yesterday?"

"Yeah, the first black reporter for the Telegram!"

"Wow. That's awesome! How'd you pull that off?"

"I just called him," Carla said. "Never had anything to call him about before. He said he heard about you and was going to reach out to arrange an interview anyway. Leo, he is such a nice guy. I can't wait to meet him."

"Yeah, you told me that yesterday."

Watching her eyes sparkle, Leo felt a brief twinge of jealously. He'd give anything to have her react to him that way.

He asked, "When is the interview?"

"Today! He's meeting us at City Hall; wants to get some pictures of you on the front steps."

"That's a great idea," Leo said, imagining the photo-op. "That'll make me look like a real contender."

"*Exactly*!" Carla said. "Okay, I'll be over here if you need me," she told him before returning to her desk.

Ruby smiled at her boss when they were alone again. When she heard Carla initiate another phone call, she told him, "That girl's a fireball. Pretty cute, too."

"Yeah." Leo nodded and sighed. "You're right on both accounts."

The council meeting was uneventful. The members voted on whether a stop light was needed at the intersection of Rosedale and Magnolia, and they opened bids for a new community center on the north side. The stop light was unanimously approved, and the construction bid went to a company Leo had never heard of. Although he found the meeting boring, he paid attention to all the little nuances.

He noticed Councilman Pratt voted for a construction company that no one else had confidence in. Leo wondered if he'd been bribed to do so; if this was one of the reasons Carla felt Mario was corrupt. Other than that, Leo felt a lot of the council members were focused on *him*. Their eyes certainly kept drifting in his direction. Maybe this was because only a few visitors bothered to attend the meeting. Or it might have been because they recognized Leo as the man who wanted to usurp the mayor's seat and integrate the schools.

After the meeting, one of the councilmen stepped down from his seat and greeted him. Leo felt he was in the presence of greatness when he shook his hand.

"Hi, I'm Dr.–"

"*Dr. Guinn,*" Leo said, shaking his hand briskly. His eyes were bright, his smile wide. "A man who needs no introduction! It's great to meet you, sir!"

Dr. Guinn was likely the most prominent Negro the city had ever known. After attending James E. Guinn Junior High (named after his grandfather), Guinn began his collegiate career at Prairie View before leaving to fight in World War II. Upon returning, he received his medical degree from the University of Texas in 1956.

Guinn established his general medicine practice in the poverty-stricken Stop-Six neighborhood in 1958 and was still the only doctor in the area. He ran for city council in 1967 and beat a white candidate by nearly ten thousand votes, becoming the first Negro to gain a position in City Hall. The LBJ administration invited him to Washington to celebrate this achievement. Guinn ran again in 1969 and was unopposed.

"It's great to meet you as well, Mr. Sullivan." Dr. Guinn was a tall man with kind eyes. "I hear you gonna give Mayor Holloway a run for his money this summer."

"Yeah," Leo said, still smiling radiantly. "That's the word on the streets. This is my campaign manager." He half-turned and smiled at Carla. "I wouldn't have known the first thing about running, if it wasn't for her. To be honest, I still don't know what I'm doing."

Carla stepped forward and shook the doctor's hand. "It's an honor to meet you, Dr. Guinn. You're a pillar of the community, a shining example of what I want my students to achieve."

"You're a teacher?"

"Yes, sir. At I.M. Terrell."

"I graduated from Terrell," Guinn said.

"Yes, sir," Carla said, beaming. "We have your picture on the wall in the main hallway."

"I used to pass it every day," Leo stated. "That portrait inspired me to go to college and make something of myself."

"Glad to hear it," Dr. Guinn said. "I'm excited to hear about any black man *or woman* who strives to be the best they can be – whatever the profession. But I gotta ask, what made you decide to run for mayor? I don't want to discourage you, but you have to know the odds are not stacked in your favor."

"It wasn't something I planned," Leo said honestly. "I spoke with some members of the community about getting the schools integrated, and we decided it probably wouldn't happen until we got new leadership – at the very top. From what I understand, Mayor Holloway could get those schools integrated by fall, if he chose to."

"That is true," the doctor said, nodding.

"I know I'm a longshot," Leo stated. "But I've got a lot of people backing me. We believe we can make a difference."

"He can do it," Carla said. "Everyone loves Leo. I think most of the people in this city want to have integrated schools."

"But *you*, sir," Leo said, "I don't think anyone would disagree that you'd make a *much* better candidate. You actually have political experience – and a bigger name. You're a living legend."

Leo felt Carla would take offense to him trying to pass the buck yet again, so he didn't dare look her way.

"Politics is not really my game," the doctor said, shaking his head. "In fact, I'm not going to seek reelection when my term is up."

This news came as a shock to Leo and Carla.

"I joined the city council with a particular agenda," the doctor said, "and I've been fortunate enough to accomplish most of my goals. The living conditions for our people are still not optimal, but things are better than they were before I arrived. The fact is, I'm a doctor, and I'd rather care for my patients in an exam room. I've never liked these stuffy meetings."

It was still disheartening to know he wouldn't be on the city council after next year, but Leo understood.

"Have you gained support from the GLL?" Dr. Guinn asked Carla.

She shook her head. "I'm trying, but I think they're dead set on endorsing Holloway."

"What's the GLL?" Leo asked.

"The Good Government League," the doctor said. "A lot of the big businesses downtown came together to create the group. They're so influential, almost nothing gets done in this city unless they approve. I wouldn't have made it to the city council without their blessing."

Again Leo was staggered by how little he knew – about everything, it seemed.

"I have some contacts in the group," Dr. Guinn told Carla. "I'll reach out to them, see what I can do."

"Thank you!" she replied. "We'd really appreciate that."

"Good luck to you," Guinn said and shook Leo's hand again. "Good luck to you both."

Another man approached Leo and Carla when they left the council chamber. This one was a stranger.

"Mr. Sullivan."

They turned to see a young black man toting a notepad and camera.

"Hi. I'm Cecil Johnson, from the Telegram. I spoke with Miss Hunter about interviewing you today."

"Oh, hi!" Leo said, reaching to shake his hand. He'd noticed the reporter was one of the visitors who had attended the council meeting. He was happy to see the man was shorter than he was and not as attractive – not that he was jealous or anything.

"Mr. Johnson! What a pleasure to meet you!" Carla said. "I'm a big fan of your work!"

"She's been dying to meet you," Leo told him.

"I have," Carla confirmed. "You're another hometown hero. We just spoke to Dr. Guinn. I feel like I'm at the Negro Hall of Fame!"

The reporter chuckled. "Please, call me Cecil. And I haven't done anything remarkable – other than get a job. Let me get a Pulitzer or two under my belt, before you go overboard." He was a fair-skinned gentleman with bold-framed glasses and a quick smile. "I can interview you at your office," he told Leo. "I'd like to get a few pictures of you out front, before we head that way."

"Sounds good," Leo responded, and they got moving again.

"I love the story you did on the poverty rate in the projects," Carla told him. "The city tries to sweep that whole segment of society under the rug. They'll forget about them altogether, if we let 'em."

"That was a tough story," Cecil recalled. "Some of the things I learned while I was speaking to those families will haunt me for years..."

Outside the sun was bright, and the sidewalk was mostly deserted; providing perfect conditions for the photo-op. Cecil positioned Leo right outside the front doors of City Hall and backed away to take a few pictures. He then asked Carla to stand next to him, thinking it would be a good idea to capture the candidate and his campaign manager.

"Y'all look good together," Cecil said as he snapped the pics. "Move in a little closer, if you don't mind..."

Leo didn't mind at all. He hoped the reporter would ask him to wrap his arm around Carla's waist, but he didn't.

A minute later, Cecil had all the pictures he needed. By then a small crowd had gathered to see what was going on.

"Thank you," Cecil told Leo and Carla. Noticing the bystanders, he removed a notepad from his breast pocket and said, "So, tell me, Mr. Sullivan, what made you decide to run for mayor?"

"I thought we were doing the interview at the office..."

"*Ah-hem.*" Carla cleared her throat much louder than was necessary.

Leo looked her way, and she casually gestured towards the dozen or so people who had gathered around them.

"Oh," Leo said. "*Oh...*" His eyes brightened. "Um, could you repeat the question?" he said to the reporter.

Cecil was all for it. "Sure. What made you decide to run for mayor?"

Leo had not prepped for a speech, but he was accustomed to standing before a jury box, trying to persuade a courtroom to see things his way.

"Running for mayor is not something I wanted to do – not initially. I'm a lawyer by profession. I've never been a politician. While some might see that as a fault, I see it as one of the best things I have going for me. I'm not a politician, so it will never be business as usual with me. I'm *incorruptible.* I'm just a regular Joe who saw a need for change and realized *I* have to be the catalyst for that change."

"What change do you feel is needed?" Cecil asked, egging him on.

Leo looked around and saw the crowd was getting larger by the second. He forced his expression to remain as serious as the topic at hand.

"We need change in our schools! The Supreme Court ruled against segregated schools in 1954. *Nineteen-fifty-four*! And here it is, nearly two decades later, and we still have segregated schools in Overbrook Meadows. All of our black students have *but one choice* for high school, and that's I.M. Terrell. How can this be?

"After diligently researching the matter, I realized the answer lies in this building behind me. We have segregated schools in Overbrook Meadows because City Hall is not doing its job, and Mayor Holloway wants things to remain the way they are! But that's not gonna happen!"

The eyes fixed on Leo invigorated him. His chest swelled. His speech became more fiery.

"Mayor Holloway and the Overbrook Meadows school board stand in direct opposition of the law of the land! They stand in contempt of the Supreme Court of the United States of America, and we must put an end to it! If Mayor Holloway won't do what's right and integrate our schools, we need to get rid of him! A vote for me is a vote to save our schools and our integrity!

"One day we'll all see that Holloway was on the wrong side of history and the wrong side of America. But for now, we gotta get him outta there! He doesn't deserve to be our mayor, not if he's going to break the law and keep our schools segregated!"

Leo was surprised to hear voices from the crowd cheering him on – and not just the black folks. There were over twenty people watching now.

"We gotta vote Holloway out of office to save our schools!" Leo bellowed.

"*Yeah*!" the people shouted. One of the loudest voices in agreement came from the woman standing by Leo's side.

"Get him outta there!" Carla echoed. *"Vote for Leo to save our schools!"*

Cecil was all smiles. Leo noticed the reporter's attention refocus on a position behind him, and he looked back. His mouth fell open when he saw that Mayor Holloway had exited the doors of City Hall, flanked by two city council members, both of them white. Holloway hadn't attended the meeting that afternoon, so Leo didn't think he was in the building.

Fire blazed behind the mayor's pupils when he locked eyes with the whippersnapper who was causing all the ruckus. Leo couldn't stop a snarky grin from curving his lips. Cecil quickly stepped past him, notepad in hand.

"Mayor Holloway! I'm Cecil Johnson, from the Overbrook Meadows Telegram. Would you like to comment on what Mr. Sullivan has said?"

"I'm, this…" Holloway's face grew red, right before their eyes. But he was a seasoned politician. His recovery was just as quick. "What this gentleman said is not true! I spoke with Mr. Sullivan a few weeks ago, and I told him we were in the process of integrating *all* of our schools. I'm not sure why this *lawyer* thinks we can get something like that accomplished in only three weeks, but that just goes to show you how little he understands about the way city government works. He has *zero* experience in politics, and he'd make a *terrible* mayor. Run this city into the ground, is what he'd do!"

"Why haven't the schools been fully integrated?" Cecil asked. "The Supreme Court ruled against segregated schools in 1954."

Before the mayor could respond, someone in the crowd shouted, *"White schools for whites! Nigger schools for niggers!"*

Leo was shocked but also elated when others picked up the chant.

"White schools for whites! Nigger schools for niggers!"

"What do you have to say about what your constituents are chanting?" Cecil shouted over them. "What message would you like to give these people regarding school integration?"

"It – is, *umph*..." The mayor looked like someone shoved a hot poker up his ass. "I, that's – who's to say those are my constituents? Is this on the record?"

Cecil nodded. "Yes, sir. I've identified myself as a reporter for the Overbrook Meadows Telegram."

Holloway half turned and feigned to have issues with his hearing. He raised a cupped hand behind his ear. "I'm sorry, I can't, I can't hear you. Those people, it's too loud. I can't understand what you're saying."

"I asked what you'd like to tell these people–"

"Thank you," the mayor said, backing towards the door. One of the councilmen conveniently pulled it open for him. "If you'd like to schedule an interview, please call my office." The mayor shook his head. "I'm sorry, I can't... I just can't hear you..."

With that, he hastily made his escape.

When the doors closed, Cecil looked over at Leo and Carla and smiled. "Would you like to go to your office and finish our interview now?"

"I'm sorry, I can't hear you," Leo joked. "I just –
sorry, I can't!" He shook his head, and all three of them
laughed.

CHAPTER NINE
CECIL JOHNSON

Oh, they mad
Ooh, they fuming
Face all red
Head vein bulging
They look scared
Are you scared?
Might put a price
On yo head
What you done did
To bring all this?
Fight for them kids?
Now they pissed?
All in they feelings
You ain't did nothing
That means you must
Be on to something

Leo's interview mostly consisted of questions the reporter referred to as *soft balls*. Cecil did not drill Leo on his qualifications to become mayor or his understanding of politics in general. Instead he asked about his platform, how the community had been responding to his campaign and the barriers he thought he'd encounter when it was time to integrate the schools.

Cecil only questioned Leo's political experience once, and he let him off the hook with the response Leo had been rehearsing with Carla.

"I've never worked in City Hall, but I've served my community for years as a lawyer," Leo explained. "I've taken many pro bono cases for citizens who were being railroaded by the justice system. I've helped settle land disputes. I've helped underprivileged families with unlawful evictions. I've helped some secure loans for their homes.

"As I mentioned earlier, it's actually good that I'm not your *typical politician*. I want to work for the people without any of the negative influences some politicians succumb to. No one's got me in their pocket, and that's the way I plan to keep it. I will always work only for the people of Overbrook Meadows, starting with our children. The first thing on my agenda is to shut down I.M. Terrell and integrate our schools."

Cecil thanked him for his time and wrapped up the interview. He took a few more pictures of Leo at his desk and snapped shots of Carla in her war room. Outside the office, he took more pictures of Leo in front of his place of business.

Before he took off, Cecil told him, "Thanks, Mr. Sullivan. I really appreciate you taking the time to meet with me today."

"No, I'm the one who's thankful for the interview," Leo replied. "I need all the publicity I can get, especially somewhere big like the paper."

"I'm not sure where the editors will put your story," Cecil cautioned him. "Knowing them, it might get buried somewhere in the back. But plenty of people will still see it. I hope you guys are ready for the shitstorm that's coming your way when it gets printed."

Leo raised an eyebrow. "Shitstorm?"

"Yeah," the reporter said. "Like the reaction we got at the courthouse, but on a much larger scale. People are liable to start harassing you wherever you go. They might even vandalize your law office."

"Can't say I'm prepared for that," Leo replied. "But we'll deal with it if it happens."

He looked over at Carla, and she supported him with a nod.

"No matter what obstacles you encounter," Cecil said, "I hope you won't give up. What you're doing is important. Like every other black adult in this town, I graduated from Terrell. On one hand, the school has served to bond us with culture and familiarity. But when I think about why we all went to the same school, it's a hurtful, ugly shame, like the slaves who were bonded in fear of beatings and lynchings.

"I'm sure you know your chances of taking Holloway down are slim. But don't let that discourage you from fighting. Even if you lose, the issue of school integration will be on everyone's mind in the fall. The mayor will have no choice but to act on it. If he refuses to do what's right, the people will take the fight to him, just like you're doing."

Leo nodded and shook his hand again. He'd never paid much attention to who wrote a particular article in the paper, but from that moment on, he'd seek out Cecil's contributions in the Telegram. The man was smart and insightful, and he certainly had a way with words.

"Thanks again for reporting on me – on *us*." Leo threw an arm around Carla and squeezed her shoulder. It was the first time they'd made physical contact, other than a handshake. "We appreciate everything you're doing for the community."

Leo was awakened on Wednesday morning by a phone call that beat his alarm clock by twenty minutes. He cursed the caller as he rubbed sleep from his eyes. He assumed it was a wrong number, because everyone he knew personally was well aware of how much he valued his sleep.

He reached to his nightstand and knocked the receiver off the phone's cradle in his attempt to clutch it. He leaned further off the bed and scooped the phone from the floor.

"Hello?" he muttered, ready to deliver a tongue-lashing to whoever was on the other end.

"You're wading in murky waters."

Leo frowned. He recognized the hushed voice was a white male and that was all. He barely heard what the caller had said.

"What?"

"You should drop out of the race," the stranger said, "if you know what's good for you. You keep it up, you won't even see us coming. Leave you bleeding like a stuck pig."

Leo's eyes widened. His heart froze. He shook off his sleep briskly, like a cobweb he'd mistakenly walked into.

"Who is this?" he snapped. "How'd you get my–"

The caller hung up. Moments later, a dial tone sang in Leo's ear.

He brought the receiver away from his face and stared at it for a few moments, as if the device would shed insight on who had threatened him. The sun had not fully risen in the eastern skies above Overbrook Meadows, but the room felt darker now; darker than it was before he received the call. Leo's chest began to knock, as his anger fought fright for the upper hand.

He hung up the phone and sat up, listening to the stillness of his home. When he was convinced there was no one inside, he rose to his feet and crossed the floor quickly, reaching for the light switch. The illumination confirmed what he had already surmised. He was alone in the bedroom. The shadows he'd seen a moment ago had been vanquished. Even still, it wouldn't hurt to be diligent. Leo investigated every room in his home, flipping the light switches as he went. His inspection yielded no fruit and ended where it had begun.

By then anger had won the battle in his heart and mind. How dare someone call his home and threaten him? This was an invasion of his privacy, and it was illegal. He could probably have the phone company pull the records and determine who the offender was. Did they really believe the threat would be enough to make him drop out of the mayoral race? If anything, Leo felt energized and more determined to fight against anyone who had the same state of mind of the man who had called him.

He stepped into the bathroom to wash his face before returning to the bedroom in search of his pajama top. He slipped it on and headed to the front door. The July 1st temperature was expected to surpass 100 degrees that day, but the atmosphere felt pleasant when Leo walked outside. He had to take a few steps down his sidewalk, because his paperboy's toss didn't deliver the news all the way to his porch that morning.

As he bent to scoop the newspaper from the walkway, Leo spotted something in the corner of his eye. The '62 Mercury wasn't necessarily out of place in his neighborhood, even though it was parked on the street six houses down, rather than in the driveway. And from that distance, Leo couldn't hear the car's engine idling. But the Mercury caught his attention just the same. And as he stared at the back windshield, the car began to slowly drive away.

Leo's next breath caught in his throat. He swallowed it down roughly, his eyes glued to the unfamiliar vehicle. The Mercury made a right at the next corner and disappeared from sight. Leo was never able to determine the sex or race of the driver. The temperature dipped ten degrees as he rose to his full height, his newspaper in hand. His heart began to knock again. This time the tendrils of fear overpowered his annoyance.

He looked in the opposite direction and didn't see anything awry. All of the cars were in the driveways, and he recognized them as his neighbor's vehicles. He looked back towards his house, half expecting to see a masked man standing in the doorway. The intruder had somehow sneaked in behind him, in the short time it took him to retrieve the paper. Or maybe the prowler had been inside his home the whole time; hiding under the bed, one of the places Leo failed to check.

But there was no one standing in his doorway.

Leo's bare feet quickly returned him to his humble abode, as it as certainly safer inside than out. He locked the door and headed straight for his bedroom closet. Inside, he found his Browning .20 gauge leaning against the wall. Back in the bedroom, he had a box of shotgun shells in his nightstand.

He hadn't loaded the weapon in well over a year, but once he remembered where the first shell went, the next five slid in smoothly. He cocked the gun, something his father told him to never do (a) inside a home and (b) unless he was ready to fire it, but Leo legitimately felt his life was in danger. As a concession to his late father, he made sure the gun's safety was engaged before he placed it on the bed and sat next to it.

With his equalizer armed and ready, he felt considerably better. He didn't feel *great*, but he no longer felt like a sitting duck. His attention returned to the newspaper, which he'd tossed on the bed before going for his shotgun. Even with the paper rolled, he saw something on the front page that kicked his stressed heartbeats up another notch. When he removed the rubber band and spread the paper on his lap, everything that had happened that morning suddenly made sense.

Cecil had worried the Telegram's editor might bury his story somewhere in the back of the paper. That was not the case. On the front page, Cecil's headline was bold and blaring.

SULLIVAN CAMPAIGNS TO INTEGRATE SCHOOLS

Beneath the headline was a picture of Leo and Carla, taken on the steps of City Hall. Leo was too anxious to read the article. He left the bedroom and found his briefcase in the den. He searched for a number he knew he had tucked away and was fortunate to find it in less than a minute. He returned to the bedroom and placed his call.

Carla answered after four agonizingly long rings. But she sounded fully awake.

"Hello?"

"Hey, it's me, Leo."

"Oh, hi. What's, what's going on? I was just getting ready for work now."

Even in his state of distress, Leo was delighted to hear that she referred to his campaign as her job.

"Did you see the paper?" he asked.

"No. It should be on the porch. Did our story get printed?"

"Yeah."

"What's wrong? Did they mess it up – or hide it way in the back? Hold on."

"*Wait.*"

Leo wanted to warn her not to go outside, but she had already put the phone down. He waited for what felt like an eternity for her to return to the line. A few horrible scenarios attempted to infiltrate his mind, but he forced the thoughts away.

She picked up the phone and said, "*Oh my God, Leo!* We got the front page! Look at that headline, and that picture! This is *huge!*"

"Yeah, and it's already attracting some negative attention."

"What do you mean?"

He told her about the phone call and the car on his street. Her excitement had fizzled by the time he was done speaking.

"Okay," she said. "What do you wanna do? Did you call the police?"

"What good would that do?" Leo wondered. "There's nothing illegal about a car parked on my street."

"But the threat..."

"I'll report it when I get to the office," he told her. "In the meantime, I think we should take these things seriously. If you're still coming to the office today, I don't want you to come alone."

"Why wouldn't I come to the office?"

"I don't know. Maybe you're spooked."

"They can't stop me from fighting for what's right," she said. "But what about you? You're the one they're targeting."

"They can't stop me either," Leo assured her. "I want you to ride with me this morning. I can be there in forty-five minutes."

He thought she might remind him of how well she could take care of herself.

Instead she simply said, "Okay, Leo. I'll be ready."

CHAPTER TEN
A SOFTER SIDE

Carla answered the door wearing a sleeveless blouse with a skirt that actually stopped above her knees; not by much, but enough to make Leo's eyes dilate. Her arms and legs were silky smooth. Her afro was perfect. As was her norm, she was beautiful without any makeup.

"Morning," he told her. "You ready?"

She nodded. "Yeah. Let me grab my lunch."

He watched her as she turned and stepped away from the door. Her slim waist seemed to beg for one of his hands on either side. He wondered if he would ever touch her in that manner. He supposed he could, or at least find out if he could, if he ever built up the nerve to ask her out. But he feared it would ruin their work relationship, especially if she rejected him. It might be impossible to get past the awkwardness.

She returned and asked him, "So, did you see any weirdos hanging around my house?"

"No. I circled the block to make sure."

She locked the door and then turned to face him. "Did you really?"

"Yeah, I did." When they got to his car, he went around to open the door for her.

"What would you have done if you saw someone?" she wondered.

He closed the door and saved his response until he got behind the wheel.

"I would've confronted them, asked why they were there."

"Do you have a weapon of some sort?"

He nodded. "I got my shotgun in the trunk. Can't remember the last time I felt the need to travel with it."

"A lot of good it'll do us in the trunk."

He looked over at her and noticed she was smiling.

"Why do I feel like you're not taking me seriously?"

"Kinda hard to go from the Leo I've known to the gun-toting bodyguard you've become."

"What about my transition from mild-mannered attorney to mayoral candidate? Is that hard to accept too?"

She looked him in the eyes, still grinning. "No. I think you've always been an activist at heart."

"But not a bodyguard?"

"I suppose every man has his own set of protective instincts," she said, staring out of the window now.

"I will protect you," Leo assured her.

"Hopefully you won't need to."

"I hope so too. I'm still a little rattled about those guys who were on my street."

"What do you think they wanted?"

"To see if I really lived there?" he offered. "Maybe to study my routine."

"For what purpose?"

He shrugged. "I guess it's not *murder*, 'cause they could've done that."

She turned his way again. "Don't talk like that."

"You're the one who filled my head with those civil rights horror stories."

"Are you frightened?"

"I'm more upset than afraid."

"You haven't considered backing down?"

"What, you mean back out of the race?"

She nodded.

"Is that what I told you this morning? *'Oh, I'ma scared. I think we should call the whole thing off!'* Or did I tell you I wanted to come pick you up, so we can go to work?"

She smiled. "You said you wanted to pick me up."

"Damn right."

"Well, I'm not saying I didn't like the old Leo, but I *really* like this new one."

Her comment left him momentarily tongue-tied. By the time he came up with a flirty comeback, they were a mile down the road, and his opportunity had passed.

At the office, Carla quickly got down to the serious business of campaigning. Leo wished he could offer as much of an effort, but he still had a law practice to run. A couple of his clients were starting to feel neglected, and he had to be in court for most of the morning.

When he returned at lunchtime, he was surprised to see Carla's war room was fully operational. The unfamiliar cars parked outside gave him pause, and he heard the chatter the moment he stepped inside. He approached his campaign manager's office and saw her along with four other women seated at two long tables. All of the ladies were on the phone soliciting donations, jotting down names and numbers on identical notepads.

They paid him no mind, so he backed out and walked to his secretary's desk.

"When did they get here?"

"Not long after you left," Ruby replied.

"Who are they?"

"Members of your campaign team. You don't know them?"

"I may have seen a couple of them at the church."

"Carla says they all work at Terrell. With school out for the summer, they have time on their hands."

Leo nodded. He wondered if they would normally pick up shifts at a department store, like Carla said she would.

"You should've seen the way she got them organized," Ruby commented. "She's a natural."

Leo nodded. "Every day I'm more impressed with her."

In his office, he tried to focus on his legal work and solicit a few donations himself, but it was hard to remain focused. The conversations in the adjacent office didn't bother him. It was Carla who held his attention hostage. Each time she spoke, on the phone or to her group, Leo strained his ears, trying to catch every word.

Ruby was right about her organizational and leadership skills. Carla instructed her team as if she'd been running campaigns for years. She cheered on their success and encouraged them when they became disheartened. Overall, Leo heard more cheers than the latter. It seemed like every few minutes one of the ladies told a caller, "Thank you! We really appreciate your support!"

Towards the end of the day, he and Ruby were discussing a troublesome client when Carla appeared in his doorway.

"Excuse me, are you busy?"

"No," Leo told her. "Come on in."

She cradled a ledger against her chest, grinning broadly. "Today has been a great day."

"Sounds like it," Leo said. "Your girls have been making calls nonstop."

"They're awesome, aren't they?"

"They are. I'm humbled by the work they're doing on my behalf."

"Guess how much we've got in donations," she said, looking down at her numbers.

Leo smiled. He liked this playful side of Carla.

"I can't imagine. On Monday you said we were up to six thousand, right?"

She nodded. "Yep."

"I wouldn't think you've got much more than that in only a couple of days..."

"We got $3,000 in just *one* day," Carla announced.

"You did not."

"Yes, sir, we did!"

"That's amazing! Is it because we have more callers?"

"It wasn't just the ladies," Carla said. "Almost everyone who gave a donation today said they saw you in the paper. Some of them even called *us*, offering to give."

"That's true," Ruby told Leo. "I transferred the calls to your campaign team."

Leo's smile was as big as Carla's. "They're calling us now? I thought we'd get more negative reactions to that article."

"Oh, we got plenty of those too," Carla informed him. "One guy told me, *'If you calling about that nigger what was on the newspaper, you need to lose my number!'*"

Leo and Ruby laughed at her impersonation.

"But that wasn't the typical response," Carla said. "Most people were eager to do what they could to help. Some of the ones who couldn't afford to donate promised to come to the church this Sunday to volunteer their time."

"I hope they'll show up in time to hear Pastor Warren's sermon," Leo joked.

"I can't promise that. Oh, and I got you a meeting with a few members of that GLL group Dr. Guinn was talking about."

Leo's eyes widened. "Really? They wanna meet me?"

"Yes, but let's not get our hopes up. The man I spoke to said they would rather pressure Holloway to integrate the schools, instead of replacing him."

"Did he say why?"

"Actually, he did. He was pretty upfront. He said they've been working with Mayor Holloway for years, and they knew what they were getting. With you, they know you wanna integrate the schools, but other than that, you're a mystery."

"Sounds like Cecil was right about integration becoming a hot topic, whether I win or lose."

"Yeah, but let's focus on you winning," Carla said. "Putting pressure on Holloway isn't guaranteed to integrate the schools, but getting you elected will."

"You know I'm in it for the long haul," he said. "How late are you and your team staying?"

"We're about done for the day," she told him. "We'll be leaving in a few minutes."

"Let me finish up here with Ruby, and I'll be there in a second. I wanna thank them for volunteering their time."

"Okay."

Before she exited the room, Leo said, "I'm giving you a ride home, right?"

"Oh, well I'm sure one of my friends can take me."

"But I *want* to. I don't think we're in the clear, as far as those threats are concerned."

"Okay," she said and repeated what she told him the first time he insisted: "If it'll make you feel better."

"It will."

When they were alone, Ruby said, "I see you've taken a liking to that woman."

Leo sighed. "Is it that obvious?"

"Stevie Wonder could see it. You plan on asking her out?"

"I was thinking about it this morning. I don't wanna do anything to mess up what we got going here. If she shoots me down, things will get weird. If she doesn't, it could get complicated."

"And if she runs into Prince Charming tonight and lives happily ever after, you'll kick yourself for letting the opportunity pass you by."

He frowned. "Now why would you go and say something like that?"

"If we're living in the world of possibilities, might as well consider all of 'em, right?"

"No. Actually, I'd prefer not to."

She chuckled. "Okay, Leo. I'm out of it. I've given my two cents, and I'll leave it alone. I probably shouldn't have said anything, but I've known you for a long time. It pains me to see you suffer."

Leo didn't think that was an accurate observation, but he couldn't deny the longing in his soul had reached the point of heartache.

"Thanks, Ruby. You're always right."

"Not always."

"Well, you're certainly right about this."

On the way to Carla's house, Leo was mostly silent. Initially his passenger was oblivious to his change in demeanor. She continued to harp on the success of the day and her goals for tomorrow. When they neared her home, she finally stopped speaking and stared at him.

"What's the matter, Leo? Aren't you excited about any of this?"

"Yeah. I am. It's, uh, it's really cool."

"*Really cool?*" She chuckled. "I guess... I think I'd be a little more animated, if I had a bunch of white folks rooting for me to become mayor."

"Sorry," he said. "I guess I'm distracted."

"I can tell. Wanna tell me what's on your mind?"

He took a deep breath and said, "It's you."

"*Me?* What did I do?"

He grinned. "Nothing. You didn't do anything wrong, just being you."

She frowned. "So what's the problem then? You're not paying me, so I know you're not about to ask me to take a pay cut."

He laughed. "That's what I'm talking about."

"Are you purposefully talking in riddles, or am I a little dense?"

"Sorry. I don't mean to be confusing. I usually don't have a hard time telling a woman how I feel about her."

He looked over at her, and Carla's eyes widened briefly.

"Oh," was all she could say.

"We spend a lot of time together," he went on. "But I long for something different. I wanna see you away from work and talk about things unrelated to the campaign. I wanna get to know you, on a personal level." He took another deep breath and blew it out silently before asking, "Do you think that might be something you're interested in, going out to dinner sometime?"

His heart squeezed like a vice, until a slight smile curved her full lips. "Sure, Leo. When would you like to take me to dinner?"

His smile was twice the size of hers. "We can go tonight; right now, if you want."

She looked up and noticed he had pulled onto her street.

"You wait till we get all the way here before asking? Do you know how many nice restaurants we passed between your job and my house?"

"I do," Leo said with a chuckle, "and I apologize. I know of a great place not far from here. We'll be there in no time."

He took her to a quaint, little steakhouse on Bridge Street that was sparsely populated on a Wednesday night. Avoiding conversating about the mayoral race was initially difficult, as this was the fire that had united them. But Leo was interested in making other connections. He talked about his law office; entertaining her with the story of a husband who hired him for three separate divorces – all from the same woman.

"Why in the world did he keep remarrying her?" Carla wondered.

"They kept having children while *on break*," Leo recalled. "They thought they should get back together for the sake of the family."

Carla, in turn, spoke about her deepest passion. Between grade school and his college days, Leo had plenty of teachers who loved what they did. But listening to Carla, he felt like he was listening to Smokey Robinson explain what music meant to him.

They drank wine and were in excellent moods when their waitress delivered the check. But it seemed no matter how hard Leo tried to leave the campaign out of their first date, they couldn't escape the polarizing nature of his efforts.

He had noticed a table of three white men in the restaurant. They seemed to recognize him, most likely from his picture in the paper. But they didn't do anything other than steal glances at him and Carla while they dined, so Leo didn't mention it. Carla had her back to them, and she was happy, and that was the way he wanted to keep it.

Unfortunately, the white diners headed for the exit immediately after the black couple. Leo did not consider the timing coincidental. He remained wary, even as Carla skipped down the front steps, her head in the clouds.

"Y'all them agitators from the paper."

Leo turned slowly, his teeth clenched, the taste of war on his lips.

Unlike the first group of boys who had accosted them, these men were in their mid-forties. Their dress was office casual. Leo could smell the alcohol on their breaths from ten feet away, especially the aggressor, who took a staggering step towards him.

"Niggers need to stay in their own damn school!"

The man brought a hand up and pointed at Leo's face, as if his finger was a magic wand that would make Negroes obey on command.

Leo balled his fists and met the troublemaker head on, unconcerned with the fact that he was outnumbered. But thankfully cooler heads prevailed. The drunkard's friends rushed forward and restrained him.

"Hey, cut it out, Kevin!"

As was the case with most cowards, Kevin fought hard to free himself, once it was clear his friends weren't going to let him get in a fight.

"I'll kick your ass!" The man worked himself into a frenzy, until his face was red, and spittle flew from his mouth. "Mayor Holloway's a good man! A nigger'll never be mayor! You hear me? *Never!*"

Leo's nostrils flared. His pulse quickened. He wanted to coldcock him, even while his friends were holding him. Instead he recalled the advice his mother had given him regarding situations like this.

When they go low, you go high.

Unless it was self-defense, she was always against Leo fighting. She felt a real man could handle disputes with his brain and his words. It was this thinking that led Leo to enroll in law school. With Mama on his mind, he relaxed his hands. He tore his eyes away from the Tasmanian devil and looked at the men gripping his arms.

"Thank you," Leo said. "I appreciate your help."

"Ain't doing it for you," the one on the right spat. "Just don't want my brother to go to jail tonight. You ain't worth it. Your coon-ass will *never* be mayor."

"Mayor of Africa, maybe," the one on the left said with a chuckle.

"You best get out of here," the first one warned, "'fore we decide to turn 'em lose."

His sinister grin made Leo ball his fists again, but a soft hand gripped his wrist at that moment. He turned and saw a beautiful, brown angel standing by his side.

Carla smiled and said, "Come on, baby."

Leo was stunned, both by the fact that she called him *baby* and the way she worked her hand into his, until their fingers were interlaced. He followed her down the steps, his heart light in his chest. The knuckleheads behind him meant absolutely nothing at that moment. They could've been a figment of his imagination.

When they got to Carla's place, Leo walked her to the door but didn't attempt to go inside. He felt bad about the way their date had ended, but she remained upbeat.

"I'm sorry," he told her. "I wish we could go somewhere without–"

Before he could react, she wrapped her arms around his waist and stepped in for a kiss. He barely had time to close his eyes before her soft lips were on his. He saw lightening behind his closed eyelids when their lips touched, but it was over much too quickly.

She backed away and smiled. "My hero."

The look in her eyes made Leo's heart flutter. He grinned sheepishly as she turned to unlock her door. She looked back at him when she got it open.

"You don't have anything to apologize for."

Before she stepped inside, he reached for her hand.

"Wait."

He pulled her to him, until her breast pressed against his. Her breath caught when he leaned down to kiss her; much slower than she had done. He had time to savor the feel of her lips, her scent, her heartbeats. He sucked her bottom lip into his mouth as his hand moved to the small of her back. He pulled her closer still, until there was no space between their hips.

She placed a hand on his chest and gently pushed him away. Leo allowed her to flee his embrace. Her eyes were drunk with passion as she backed into the darkness of her home. Once again, Leo felt like he had the upper hand. He was bold and self-assured.

"When you called me baby at the restaurant, was that to get me to calm down?" he asked.

She nodded, smiled. "Yeah. And it worked."

He said, "Sure would like to hear you call me that more often."

"Keep putting a smile on my face," she advised him, "and I'm sure it'll happen. Are you picking me up for work tomorrow?"

He nodded, his grin widening.

"See you then," she said. "Goodnight, Mr. Sullivan."

She closed the door, and Leo stood guard for thirty seconds before floating down the steps, his head in the clouds this time.

CHAPTER ELEVEN
OPPOSITION

From the jungles
You've been delivered
No more arrows in quivers
No more knuckle dragging
Spear-chucking
Dodging crocodiles as you bathe in the river
You've been delivered
Given religion
The white man has saved your soul
Even freed you from bondage
Over a hundred years ago
But you want more
It's not enough
No, it's never enough
Gave you the fountains
The right to vote
But for you
It's never enough
Now our schools?
Not this time!
All you do is take
You've made it clear

Why don't you take
Your ass back to Africa
If you don't like it here

On Sunday, Leo and Carla arrived early enough to catch the full service at Ebenezer Baptist Church. To their delight, the church was more populated than they had ever seen it. Generally, Pastor Warren could count on a hundred faithfuls to fill his pews on Sunday morning. That day, there were well over 150 people there, and the pastor was in rare form. He delivered a passionate sermon about forgiveness that had everyone checking their heart to see if they were living up to God's plan for their lives.

After church, almost all of the attendees headed to the cafeteria. When Leo entered, the overwhelming show of support brought tears to his eyes. His campaign team included over two dozen white people now. Leo noticed some of Pastor Warren's most reliable parishioners, older women who had been coming to the church for years, finally decided to stick around this afternoon. Whether it was out of curiosity or sincere support of his cause, Leo was grateful to have them.

"Thank you all for coming. We have a lot to do today, so everyone please take a seat so we can get started."

With so much excited energy in the room, it took a minute to get them settled down, but eventually they quieted.

"First of all, I can't express how grateful I am to see all of you here," Leo said. "It seems like only a couple of weeks ago we had our first meeting in this cafeteria. We came together with a common goal, and everything moved so quickly; like a snowball rolling downhill. That snowball has turned into a mighty avalanche, and you're all part of the force we wield today!"

His comment drew cheers from the crowd.

"The whole city is taking us seriously now," Leo continued. "Mayor Holloway definitely is."

The group grumbled their disapproval for the villain.

"I see some of you brought Wednesday's newspaper with you," Leo said, looking around the room. He couldn't help but smile at the sight of his picture on the front page. "Isn't that great? We couldn't have paid for that kind of publicity!"

"I want mine signed!" someone yelled.

"Me too!" another person said. "That's why I brought mine. I want your autograph!"

Leo chuckled. "Wow. Now I know how Marvin Gaye feels! I'd be honored to sign your papers, but first we need to get down to the business at hand. A lot of you have brought your poster boards with you. I see a lot of markers out there and paint cans. And you brought some little ones too!" His eyes twinkled at the pint-size activists.

"That's excellent, because this is all for them," Leo stated. "I hope you youngsters know you're taking part in *history* right now. All those things you've been hearing about and seeing on TV, with the civil rights movement – it's taking place right now in Overbrook Meadows, and you're a part of it. You should be very proud of yourself!"

Some of the older kids recognized the significance of their presence. You could see the gravity in their bright, eager eyes.

"I'm gonna turn the meeting over to Miss Hunter now," Leo said. "Anyone who's been involved with this campaign knows she's the brains behind this operation."

He took a step back, and the woman standing by his side beamed as she stepped forward. Her eyes were as wide as her smile.

"Oh my goodness, where did all of you wonderful people come from?! When Leo first announced his candidacy, they said we had no chance of winning. We started with a pocket full of hope and a handful of dreams. Now the donations are rolling in, and even better, the people are too! This is what a grassroots organization looks like!"

When they began to applaud, she clapped too.

"Yes, you deserve it! Give yourselves a hand!"

When the adulations died down, she said, "Now, you know we're still fighting our way uphill, and the opposition is *fierce*. We have to double-down our efforts, if we're gonna have *any* chance of beating Holloway. Today we'll start making those signs we talked about, and hopefully we can start posting them throughout the city when we leave here."

"I printed some flyers," someone said.

Carla spotted the man near the middle of the room. "Really?"

"Yeah, they're eight-by-ten," the stranger said. "I'm Brendon Foster, from Foster's Printing."

He held up one of the flyers. It was fairly basic; white background with "**LEO FOR MAYOR**" in bold, red lettering. It was a huge donation, especially considering it was unsolicited, and Brendon Foster was white.

"I brought five thousand of 'em," he said. "Figured we can start putting 'em on telephone poles and what not."

Amidst the *oohs* and *wows* from the crowd, Carla brought a hand to her mouth. "Oh my God, thank you! That is such an awesome contribution! Those flyers are gonna give us tons of visibility!"

She sniffled, or at least that's what it sounded like from Leo's perspective. But he was standing behind her and couldn't see her face.

"Mildred, Chelsea, Jackie, please stand," Carla said. When they did, she said, "If you have any questions about what to write on your signs, speak to myself or one of these women. And if today is your first day attending our meetings, and you want to get involved, please make sure I get your name and phone number before you leave. Alright, are y'all ready to make some campaign signs?"

They all responded affirmatively. "*Yeah!*"

"Well get to it!"

The room erupted in activity, and Carla took a moment to get her emotions under control. She turned towards Leo and took a deep breath. Her eyes were watery. Her smile was adorable. She mouthed the words "*Five thousand!*" and a tear rolled down her cheek. Leo ached to wrap his arms around her, even though he knew these were happy tears.

She wiped her eyes and took another deep breath. She smiled at him and then turned back towards the crowd. Their private moment lasted seven seconds, but it felt much shorter. Leo longed for so much more.

He wanted to find a group to paint posters with, but Carla said it was important for Leo to make his way through the room and greet everyone; shake their hand or hug them and thank them for coming to the meeting. Plus he had all of those newspapers to sign. He was obedient to her instructions.

One of the deacons was the first to notice something troubling. He notified the pastor, who came to give Leo a heads up. The mood in the cafeteria was loud and joyful. Pastor Warren pulled Leo aside, hoping not to disturb the positive vibes. From across the room, Carla noticed Leo's disposition change as he huddled with the preacher. He looked up and spotted her in the crowd. They locked eyes, and a chill tiptoed down Carla's spine.

She broke away from the woman she was speaking to and approached Leo and the pastor.

"What's wrong?"

"Got some trouble outside," Leo told her. "Pastor Warren says some folks are out there protesting."

"*Protesting*?" Carla frowned. "Protesting *here*? What are they protesting?"

"Deacon Murphy's out there now trying to get a better look at their signs," Pastor Warren said. "But he said it's got something to do with the schools."

Carla shook her head in bewilderment. "What, why would they be protesting here?"

"Seems they got word about the good work you guys are doing here," Pastor said. "Maybe they're gearing up for what's to come; trying to nip it in the bud, before things go any further."

Carla watched Leo's eyes, which had transitioned from confusion to anger.

"What are you gonna do?" she asked him.

"I'm going out there, to see what they want."

"I'll go too," Carla said right away.

On the way out of the side entrance, they ran into Deacon Murphy. He was a tall man, with skin as dark as molasses.

"Find out why they're here?" the pastor asked him.

"They're protesting your campaign," the deacon said to Leo. "A bunch of hate out there. They don't want those schools integrated."

"You talked to them?" Leo asked. "What do they think coming here will solve?"

The deacon shook his head. "I didn't talk to them. They're on the property, but not too close to the church. I didn't wanna go down there – not by myself."

Leo's heart kicked uncomfortably as he stepped outside and was met with bright sunlight, fierce July heat. Ebenezer Baptist was set atop a relatively tall hill. The pastor's home was fifty yards away. The property was enclosed by a ranch style wooden fence that was only waist high. The closest street was at the bottom of the hill, 100 yards in the distance.

The protestors had made their way onto the property but for some reason decided not to come all the way to the church's parking lot. Their cars were parked alongside the curb. They had encroached upon the sacred grounds by foot. From that distance, Leo couldn't make out much, only that they were all white, they numbered less than twenty, and some carried signs. He continued walking in their direction, with Carla on his left. The pastor and deacon kept up on his right.

Upon seeing him, the protesters began to speak amongst themselves and then to him directly. Their chant wasn't unified, but Leo got the gist of what they were saying. It wasn't surprising or even new material at this point. They boasted that he'd never become mayor, and white schools were for whites.

Leo tried not to let it get to him, but the fact that they would bring their hateful message to the church was infuriating. There were women and children inside – innocent people.

He continued to march forward. The crowd did as well. Adrenaline flooded his veins. It collided with the hot summer heat, momentarily making him lightheaded.

"I don't want any of the volunteers to see this," he told Carla.

"It's not about what you want," she replied gruffly. "It's about what *they* want. They didn't come to protest you, Leo. They could've done that at your office. They came to intimidate the people who are helping us, because they know we're nothing without them."

That observation angered Leo even more.

"Stay calm," Carla warned him. "We don't need hotheads on both sides."

Leo's group came to a stop in the middle of the field, when they were within 25 yards of the protesters. The angry mob did the same. They were close enough to hear their hate speech now and read their signs. Leo's senses were bombarded with the ugly truth of how some in his community viewed him and his people. It was disheartening to see how little progress they'd made since the sixties.

A few signs read, "**HOLLOWAY FOR MAYOR**."
Others were more direct: "**VOTE NO TO
INTEGRATION**," "**KEEP TEXAS WHITE**," and "**STOP
THE RACE MIXING**." The most interesting one read,
"**CURSED IS THE MAN WHO INTEGRATES –
JEREMIAH 11:3-6**."

Pastor Warren must have zeroed in on that one too.
He told Leo, "How dare they use the word of God to support
their hatred. That verse doesn't even have anything to do
with integration. That's blasphemy, what they're doing."

He sounded angry, but when Leo looked over at him,
the pastor's features were calm. Leo returned his attention
to the people of the city he intended to govern.

"What do y'all want?" he asked, his voice loud enough
to cut through their rumbling. "What have you come here
for?"

"We're here to fight for our rights!" one of them
yelled. "Fight for our mayor!"

"We're here to fight for our children!" a woman
shouted. She was young and attractive, dressed modestly in
a knee-length dress. She looked like she could've been a
teacher herself.

"That's fine," Leo told them. "Vote for Mayor
Holloway all you want. But there's no reason for you to be
here!"

"This is a free country!" one of them shouted. "We got
a right to be here!"

"*This is private property!*" Pastor Warren countered.
"This is *my* property, and this is God's house!"

"You ain't got no business over here with that mess!"
his deacon tacked on. He looked angrier than a junkyard
dog. Leo knew Deacon Murphy would protect his pastor at

all cost. He prayed he wouldn't do anything to escalate things.

"Please," Leo said, speaking to the opposition. "Y'all need to leave. We don't want no trouble."

"Make us leave!" an agitator on the other side yelled. The man was fit, in his early twenties. He sported a buzzcut, like he was fresh out of boot camp. He appeared to be speaking directly to Deacon Murphy. *"Holloway for mayor!"* he yelled, pumping his white fist in the air. *"Holloway for mayor! Holloway for mayor!"*

His cohorts quickly picked up the chant. Their number was small, but their volume was deafening.

"Get the hell away from here!"

That voice was new, and it was one Leo recognized. Cold dread washed over him when he turned and spotted his sister approaching. His eyes grew even larger when he saw she was not alone. His volunteers were pouring out of the church. Many of them toted his newly-made campaign signs. His group outnumbered the opposition 7-to-1, but he didn't want their support at this moment.

"No – *no*..." He shook his head and met his sister head on. "Go back in the church, please. Get these children out of here."

Mildred marched past him as if he wasn't even there.

"You crackers need to get out of here!" she yelled. "This is a house of God, you heathens! Get the hell away from here!"

"Fuck you, nigger!" one of her opponents bellowed.

"Hey, watch your mouth!" Deacon Murphy shouted. "Don't disrespect my church like that! *Don't disrespect my pastor!*"

"Oh God..." The contents of Leo's stomach bubbled.

This was the very thing he had hoped to avoid. His group began to hurl more insults as they drew nearer, and the shouting match was in a full freefall. With children amongst them, his group was decent enough to be careful with their language, but the flaring tempers were steadily on the rise.

"Go back inside the church!" he pleaded to his ever-growing crowd. "We'll take care of this. Please, go back inside!"

He wasn't surprised to hear his campaign manager echo his request.

"Y'all go back inside," Carla said. She turned and tried to usher them in that direction.

"We'll take care of this!" Pastor Warren yelled over the ruckus. *"More yelling won't solve anything!"*

Leo turned to corral his sister, who was the first to cross the neutral space between the groups. It appeared she would march directly into the white faction.

"Mildred, you need to—"

He was silenced by a *SMACK!* to the side of his face that staggered him. Blinded by a bright flash of pain, he initially thought he'd been punched. But as his vision cleared, he realized the white group had not moved closer.

"They throwing rocks!" someone on his side yelled.

Leo focused on the opposition and saw the offender bend to pick up another stone. It was the man with the buzzcut. As Leo watched, he rose to his feet and reached back like a baseball pitcher. With total disregard for the women and children on Leo's side, the man hurled another rock with all his might. So far, he was the only one who had engaged in such recklessness.

Still stunned, Leo reached to the source of pain on the side of his head. His nostrils flared when he felt wetness on the growing contusion. Sure enough, he withdrew his hand and saw his fingers were coated in blood.

"*You sonofabitch*," he growled and headed straight for the man who had harmed him. He didn't make it more than a few feet before someone grabbed his arm.

"*No, Leo! Stop!*"

In the split second it took him to spin angrily and confront the peacemaker, his brain told him who the voice belonged to. His rage did not immediately subside when he stared into Carla's eyes.

"*Don't do it*," she pleaded. "That's what they want you to do! You're gonna get some of your people hurt!"

Her pained expression was matched by the tears in her eyes. Leo almost told her it wasn't him who was trying to hurt people, it was *them*! They were the ones who had come here looking for trouble. They were the ones throwing rocks!

But rationale kicked in, and he knew she was right. Just like the lunch counter protesters and freedom riders who had come before him, his cause would crumble if he resorted to the same violence his oppressors used. He didn't want any of his people to be victimized, but for the sake of the movement, he understood it had to be that way.

"*They hurt Leo!*" someone close to him yelled. "*He's bleeding! They hurt Leo!*"

The crowd quickly swarmed to confirm this.

"I'm alright," Leo said, though the blood was sliding down his neck by then. "It's alright. Don't do anything to them."

"*They throwing rocks!*" The voice came from one of the youngsters near the back of the crowd.

"They throwing rocks at us!"

"Don't do anything!" Leo yelled. He turned to his group with both hands in the air, one of them red with his own blood. *"Everybody stop and listen! Listen to me!"*

He didn't think they would, but his anguish pushed his volume to the level of a megaphone.

"Do not throw rocks back!" he yelled. *"Don't yell at them! Do not yell at them! Don't do anything! They wanna provoke us! That's why they're here! They wanna bring us down to their level, but we don't have to let them!"*

It appeared everyone was out of the church by then. Leo stood tall, surrounded by 150 of the most ardent supporters he could've hoped for. They stared at him, initially in disbelief that he would ask them to back down. But gradually they saw what Carla had seen in him all along. He was a true leader. Selfless and wise. The backdrop of racists still hurling insults as Leo literally shed sacrificial blood for them furthered the depth and greatness of this moment.

"We shall overcooome..."

The voice was small, barely cutting through the commotion. It was a sweet voice. A child. Leo didn't realize it, but this was the pastor's youngest daughter, Talia. She was a member of the youth choir. Many felt her singing was angelic.

"We shall overcoooome. We shall overcome, some daaaay..."

Tears filled Leo's eyes as his group picked up on the song. His tears mingled with his sweat, which mingled with his blood. He lowered his hands. Carla was the first to reach for his left. A woman he didn't know took hold of his right hand. They turned towards the racists and joined the child in singing the most notable civil rights song America had ever known.

"*O-oh deep in my heart, I do believe, we shall overcome some daaaay...*"

The white group seemed baffled by the singing. The aggressor stopped throwing rocks, and they reverted to their chant of "**HOLLOWAY FOR MAYOR**," but it was only 20 of them. They were completely drowned out when every one of Leo's volunteers belted their song with true emotion, passion and agony.

Leo wasn't sure how long they stood there and sang and held hands before the sheriff arrived with four more squad cars. The policemen broke up the small, white mob, asking them to vacate the premises. The segregationists did so without further incident.

When they were gone, Leo's group returned to the church's cafeteria to finish their campaign signs and flyers. By the end of the day, Leo was grateful the whites had attempted to silence his movement. His team was more determined than ever.

CHAPTER TWELVE
THE FINAL CHAPTER
COMBUSTION

The next morning Leo got an early morning phone call from Pastor Warren. The pastor's news wasn't terribly surprising, but it shook the attorney to the core. Leo sat on the side of the bed with his forearms on his knees, thinking he might vomit.

He hung up and took a minute to process the information he received before he called Carla. He could tell he'd roused her from sleep.

"Umh, hello?"

"Hey. It's me."

"What's wrong?"

Leo sighed. "They burned the church. Somebody did. It's on fire right now." Saying the words aloud rattled Leo as much as it did when the pastor told him.

"Oh my God!" She was fully awake now. "Is everybody okay?"

"The pastor and his family are fine. They didn't target the house, just the church."

"What kind of—"

"This is all my fault."

"No, Leo. Don't you dare say that."

"If it wasn't for—"

"If it wasn't for *racists* who want to disobey the law of the land and keep all of the nice things for themselves, this wouldn't have happened," Carla spat. "You are not at fault, and no one who's helping you speak up for what's right is at fault. One day God will judge everyone involved in this, and we're not the one's who'll be condemned. I don't ever want to hear you say it's your fault – not now and especially not in front of the people who support you. Do you understand me?"

Her strength was astounding. Leo's eyes burned with tears, but she was powerful enough to keep them in check.

"Okay," he managed. "You're right." He sighed. "I'm on my way to the church."

"Alright. I'll meet you there."

"You don't have to come."

"You don't tell me what to do," she said and disconnected.

Leo dressed quickly and grabbed his shotgun before he left the house. He was in a hurry, but he regretted not telling Carla to wait for him to pick her up. Then again, what were the odds that she would've listened?

On the way to the church, Leo saw over a dozen of his campaign signs planted in yards and posted on telephone poles or businesses. The success of his street team was bittersweet. When he arrived at Ebenezer Baptist, he was disgusted to see the building was still in flames. There wasn't a fire truck in sight. He didn't even hear sirens in the distance. He parked a safe distance away and left his car, shotgun in hand. The pastor's family stood on the outskirts of the parking lot watching their place of worship burn.

The sunrise was barely visible on the horizon. Dark smoke choked the morning clouds. The smell of destruction filled Leo's nostrils. The temperature was pleasant, but it grew warmer as he neared the fire.

He approached the family, who were still in their pajamas. They turned and watched him. Only the youngest was crying. The last time Leo saw Talia, she was leading his campaign team in singing *We Shall Overcome*. Seeing her with tears in her dark, beautiful eyes felt like a punch to the gut.

"Is everyone okay?" he asked. "I feel horrible about this."

"We're all fine," the pastor's wife Sophia told him. Her expression was wise and kind. The church fire danced in her pupils. "We'll weather this storm. We always do."

The pastor stepped to him, and he and Leo walked away from the others.

"I'm so sorry," Leo said, glad Carla wasn't there to admonish him. "I feel like this is my fault."

"You know better than that," Pastor Warren replied. His deep voice was nurturing, his eyes reflective.

"They wouldn't have done this if we weren't meeting here," Leo countered. "They wouldn't have come here yesterday, either."

"Hate will always find an outlet," the pastor said. "I'd much rather they take it out on the church, rather than on you or one of the others."

Leo continued to frown, but he nodded slowly.

"This church has become a symbol of progress," the pastor said. "People came here for fellowship; to take down the last vestiges of segregation in this city. Lord knows it's long overdue. But the devil will use evil people to do his will. This is how they responded to the 16th Street Baptist Church in Birmingham."

Leo winced at the memory. Seven years ago, unknown assailants (presumably members of the KKK) planted dynamite outside of the basement and detonated it on a Sunday morning. Four precious black girls died in the explosion. More than a dozen more people were injured. The bombing stunned the nation and was a turning point in the Civil Rights Movement. President LBJ signed the Civil Rights Act one year later and the Voting Rights Act in 1965.

"They bombed that church," Pastor Warren went on, "because it was the headquarters for the movement in Birmingham. That's where they met to plan a lot of those marches and sit-ins. The racists couldn't stop them with arrests. Even water hoses and dogs didn't help, so they tried to use fear: This is what happens when you go against the grain; *bombs*, four little girls dead. But even that didn't work, just like this fire won't work.

"You'll get even *more* support for your campaign, Leo – watch what I tell you. As for this church..." The pastor looked back at the burning building with a glint in his eye.

141

"We'll rebuild. This church is a symbol. They can destroy
the wood, the bricks. But everyone knows you can't destroy a
symbol. We won't let bullies intimidate us. We'll have
church on the front lawn of my home next Sunday, before we
let that happen."

His words fed Leo's soul and nourished him. "Why
has no one come yet?" he asked, turning towards the main
thoroughfare. "How did I make it here before the fire
department, the police?"

"I can speculate," Pastor Warren said, following his
gaze, "but what good is that gonna do?"

The silence in the streets confirmed they had the same
speculation. Mayor Holloway was technically the boss of the
fire and police departments. If he wanted both forces to
hang back and let the church burn to the ground, so it would
be.

Carla and a dozen more concerned citizens made it to
the crime scene before the fire department arrived. She gave
condolences to the family and then fumed with everyone else
while they waited for the first firetruck. The emergency
personnel finally rounded the corner, sirens blaring. They
sprang into action, but by then the fire had obviously gutted
the church. Flames gushed from every window, even the
steeple.

In the midst of the excitement, the pastor's oldest
daughter, Nadine, immortalized the chaos with the help of a

1965 Canon Pellix. A photo enthusiast, she lined up dozens of perfect shots; catching firemen unloading the hoses, a silhouette of her mother and father watching their church burn and the angry faces in the crowd that decried the fire department's delay.

When she approached Carla and Leo, he wasn't in the mood to take a picture. He was frustrated and distraught. Carla held him, more like a companion than a lover, and the couple drew strength from one another. Leo wore a sportscoat with a collar shirt and no tie. Her dress had spaghetti straps. Her curly afro wasn't styled perfectly, but it was still beautiful.

Leo didn't have time to look at the camera or even hold his shotgun out of view before Nadine lined up her shot, with the burning church in the background. She took a picture and told them, "Thank you," before walking away.

By the time the fire was fully extinguished, nearly a hundred people had arrived to bear witness to the tragedy. They all spoke to the pastor, who thanked them for their well wishes and assured them everything would be okay. They would rebuild, and they would be stronger. Evil would not triumph over the good people of Overbrook Meadows.

Leo was aware that most of the visitors were members of his campaign team. After consoling the pastor and his family, they looked to him for guidance. Leo wasn't big on speeches, and he didn't consider this a proper setting to fulfil

a campaign directive. But he knew he had to say *something*.
He stood before the crowd, and they gradually came together
as he spoke. Carla did not stand at his side this time. She
stood before him and listened intently to his words, as did
the others.

"I've lived in this city all my life," he said. "My mother
was born here. My grandfather was born here too. Paw Paw,
he used to tell us stories about what we called the *olden
times*." He chuckled, but there was no humor in it. "He told
us beautiful things about this city's past. He told us about
some ugly things that happened here too.

"He told us about Mayor Holloway's grandfather,
who's notoriously known for being photographed at a
lynching that took place, not too far from this church. The
man who was lynched that night was Billy Sorrell. His crime
against humanity was falling in love with a white woman,
who later claimed she was raped when they were found out.

"Holloway can say his family has changed, and this
city has changed, and as for that picture, that was a long time
ago, and we should get over it already. They're always quick
to tell us to get over it, aren't they? But they're equally quick
to remind us that white supremacy is not a thing of the past;
it's something we deal with every day. It's woven into the
fabric of this country, and it's definitely part of this city's
tapestry.

"This land we're standing on, many of you know was
once a plantation. When the slaveowners passed on,
childless, they did something that was virtually unheard of:
They gave the land to the family of former slaves who were
still tending the fields as sharecroppers. Maybe they did it
out of the kindness of their heart. Maybe it was a form of

atonement, before they went to meet their maker. We will never know.

"But what we do know is the white establishment in this city was never happy about it. I can't tell you how many underhanded schemes they concocted over the past century to try to wrestle this land away from the Warrens – especially during the population boom. Do you know how many factories they could've built on this land? A Negro doesn't deserve to have all of this. They promised us forty acres and a mule, but the thought of one of us actually obtaining it was *infuriating*.

"But the Warren family weathered the storm and held on to this land, and the pastor's father built his beloved church here. For decades Ebenezer Baptist has stood, not only as a place of worship, but as a monument to black culture, black pride, and even black power. But as we've seen in the last couple of days, nothing is sacred to a white supremacist; a segregationist. They came to this holy ground yesterday with their teeth bared, hurling rocks and insults. They returned in the wee hours of the morning and burned our church down.

"And me..." He sighed. "It's easy for me to find fault in my actions that led to this. Those white folks didn't have no problem with Pastor Warren, as long as he was preaching the gospel. But my meetings, my campaign, that's what stirred up the trouble. The fact that I'm thinking like that shows how the manipulation of white supremacists knows no bounds. They didn't lynch runaway slaves because they were evil white people. They lynched them because they were trying to run away from their rightful owners.

"How dare they seek a life of freedom? How dare they want to find their children who were sold down the river?

How dare the Warren family own so much land, when there are poor whites in this city who barely have two nickels to rub against each other? How dare we want to enforce a decree the Supreme Court made in 1954 and reaffirmed in 1955, '58, '68 and '69? How dare we want the best education for our children? *How dare we*?"

Leo paused. His chest rose and fell visibly, filling his lungs and bloodstream with the smoldering remnants of Ebenezer Baptist.

"How dare I?" he asked. "How dare *you*?"

He spotted Carla in the crowd. She was as enthralled as everyone else. He was surprised to see a lone tear slide down her cheek.

"It's easy to say you'll stand up for what's right and fight against adversity," he said, "but how many of us really will? We all saw what happened yesterday. They came right to our front door and let it be known the fight was just beginning. Like cowards, they came back under the cover of darkness and set fire to our church; our campaign headquarters. Who knows where they'll strike next. Will it be my law office? My home? *Yours*?

"I don't fault any of you, if you decide this is a little too real for you. You wanted to donate a little of your time and money, but this – fires and death threats, this isn't what you signed up for. I don't fault any of you for feeling that way. If this is the last time I see you, I want you to know that I love you, and I truly understand.

"But for those of you who do stick around," he said, frowning now, "for those of you who are upset about what happened yesterday and infuriated by what happened this morning, best believe I ain't going nowhere!"

The crowd erupted in cheers. Leo paused long enough for the applause to die down.

"You can bet your bottom dollar that I'm gonna give it my all until election day, and God willing, I'll serve this city for years to come after that! *We will integrate those schools*! The people attacking us have done nothing but bring us closer together!"

As if to illustrate this point, his people converged on him, everyone wanting to hug him or shake his hand. Carla was the only one who hung back. She admired her man from afar. She couldn't have been more proud of him.

When they left the church, Leo told her he'd follow her home. He did not ask. When they got there, he parked behind her in the driveway and followed her inside. They were both exhausted, not only from the early morning wake up calls. The full measure of the stress they'd been under for the past few weeks had finally taken its toll. Carla's sofa was comfortable, but it would not satisfy her needs. She longed to stretch out on her bed, but with Leo there, it wasn't possible to do so.

She decided etiquette didn't matter on a day like this. She walked past her couch and continued towards the bedroom, while Leo turned and locked the front door. He did not seem puzzled or curious when he turned back and saw he was alone in the front room. He followed his campaign manager's footsteps and hesitated when she disappeared inside one of the bedrooms. He heard the box spring accept her weight as she reclined on the mattress. He stepped closer and peered into the room.

Carla lie on her side in the middle of the bed. Leo hadn't noticed how much flesh her dress exposed at the church, but now it was all he could think about it. The spaghetti straps left her slender arms and smooth shoulders succulently bare. The back of the dress plunged midway down her back. Now that she was lying down, Leo realized she was braless.

She had kicked off her pumps. Leo wasn't sure why the sight of her bare feet excited him, given all of the other glorious sights available to him at that moment, but they did. His eyes swam up her legs, to the curve of her hips and the swell of her backside. She was more thin than curvy, but her body was just right for him.

He felt unsure of himself as he sat behind her on the corner of the bed.

Without looking back, she told him, "Take your shoes off, if you wanna lay down."

Leo's chest shuddered as he bent to follow her instructions. He removed his sportscoat as well; draped it over the bedpost. When he was done, he lie on the bed with her. He lie on his side and scooted forward, until her ass fit perfectly in his lap. His body grew warm instantly, with most of the heat settling between his legs. He draped an arm over her side, embarrassed that he'd become aroused, hoping she wouldn't notice. But she backed into him at that moment, and he knew she was aware.

They lie quietly for so long, he thought she'd fallen asleep. He was careful not to disturb her with his movements. He stroked her arm gently. He closed his eyes and inhaled the scent of her afro, the scent of her bed. He didn't realize he had dozed off until he felt her roll to a different position. He opened his eyes to find Carla facing him. Her eyes were open, staring into his. Her gaze was intense. He didn't recognize her expression as longing until she bit down on her bottom lip, a moment before moving closer to kiss him.

Her lips were soft, her breath warm. Leo's hand was on her side, but gradually it moved lower, until it rested on her hip. Even the feel of her panty line was enticing. Once again he was erect within a matter of seconds. She surprised him by reaching between his legs while they kissed. His eyes flashed open, but hers were still closed. She squeezed his manhood and moaned softly as she slipped her tongue into his mouth. Leo closed his eyes again and enjoyed her taste, the sensations she provided.

Carla was an excellent kisser. Every movement she made was slow and sultry. Leo wanted her so badly, he feared an eruption was imminent, as she stroked him through his pants. He was grateful for the respite when she told him, "I have a condom, in the night stand."

"Okay," he managed.

He rolled over and sat up on the side of the bed. He thought he had time to pull himself together, but she sat up with him. She spread her legs and moved in behind him, with one leg on either side of his, her breasts against his back. She reached under his arms and undid the buttons on his shirt. She planted soft kisses on the back of his neck while she worked.

Leo knew her dress had to be hiked *way* up for her to straddle him like that. He looked down and confirmed he could see her thighs, all of them. He felt the heat radiating from her moist core. He wanted to rip his shirt off, buttons be damned. But Carla's sensual pace was erotic. He savored every second.

When she unfastened the last button, he raised his arms to facilitate the shirts removal. Finally she allowed him to stand and retrieve the condom. His heart shot up in his throat when he looked back at her. Her legs remained wide open. Her panties were dark, but he could still see they were damp. He stared at her unabashedly, and she did the same. Her eyes were locked on the bulge in his slacks.

"Come here," she beckoned.

Leo seemed to float as he stepped between her legs, as if he was hypnotized. She unfastened his belt and removed it completely. She made quick work of the button and zipper that secured his slacks. She pulled his pants down with the underwear entwined. His erection sprang forward, finally free.

"*Leo*," she breathed as she stared at his pulsating member. She wrapped one hand around it and stroked slowly. "*Oh, Leo*."

Her words, coupled with her touch, was almost enough to do him in. Leo hadn't been this excited since he was a teenager. He backed away and tore the condom open. It only took him a few seconds to slide it down his shaft, but he appreciated the short separation.

He'd calmed himself when he stepped between her legs again. He placed his hands on her knees, and his fingers slid down to her hips on their own accord. He gripped her panties as she lie back on the mattress. She lifted her hips and allowed him to pull the underwear off. He tossed the panties to the floor and spread her legs slowly, marveling at her oasis. It was uncommon to find a woman who shaved her kitty as low as Carla did. Her glistening lips were too inviting. He dropped to his knees before his inhibitions could stop him. She cried out when he buried his face between her thighs.

"*Oh!*"

The move caught her completely by surprise. Her legs snapped closed reflexively, but she didn't fight him when he spread them again. He lapped her juices as if he'd been lost in the desert for days. Her pearl was already swollen. Leo sucked it majestically. Carla couldn't stop from bucking her hips into his face.

"*Oh, Leo! Damn, baby!*"

She was a wildcat. Leo rode the waves as best he could. He didn't feel like more than a few minutes passed before her whole body began to tremble.

"*Leo, I'm gonna – oh baby!*"

He coerced her climax with his tongue. She reached between her legs and rubbed his head as the tsunami rolled down her frame.

"*Oh, Leo! Leo....*"

Her taste was exotic. He could've dined for days, but his manhood throbbed with a sense of urgency. When her moans and the thrashing of her hips began to subside, he reluctantly detached and rose to his feet. Carla's eyelids fluttered as she tried to focus on him. She didn't look like she had the energy to scoot back on the bed, and he didn't want her to. He guided himself in from a standing position. Carla's eyes flashed open, and she watched him.

It felt so good to feel her tight, wet warmth, Leo could've passed out. He kept pushing, until he was fully submerged. Carla's chest hitched. Sweat glistened between her breasts.

She told him, "*Ye, yes, baby,*" when he began to pump his hips rhythmically.

Leo couldn't have responded if he wanted to.

Looking down at her, into her eyes, he understood this was as close as he would ever get to paradise on earth. There was no one who would ever fulfill him like Carla did, both physically and spiritually. He savored the smell of her essence on his lips. He revered her wisdom, determination and tenacity. He was blown away by how amazing it felt to become one with her.

If he could find the wherewithal to speak, without sounding like a blubbering idiot, he might have told her he was in love with her. But maybe it was better if he didn't say it now. Surely it would be more meaningful if he told her afterwards.

EPILOGUE

Peeling apart the layers
Of your essence
And beyond
Your passion and fears
Dissecting your perfect piece of paradise
With my tongue
Those silky, red panties are a conundrum
Why are they there?
Why have you not laid bare
Your wants and desire for eternal bliss
When it's obvious my kisses
Have your body blazing like a funeral pyre
Which is appropriate
Because I want to dead all notions that I'm not the one
Dead all memories of the men who came before me
Dead all thoughts that any man can cum after
Spread your legs and understand this is **rapture**
As your spirit leaves your body
You're unable to feel the sweat
Because your skin is numb
Your heartbeats thump
To the rhythm of my tongue
Your ass lunges from the mattress
As you grind against my face

I keep salivating
Because there's no sweeter taste
It's enough to make you scream
But I wanna make you cum
Only then will I rise to my knees
Lick my lips
And gaze upon what I've done
This masterpiece
These moist sheets
Your eyes rolled back
Jaws slack
Toes twisted like gang signs
You know you are mine
You know for certain
Even before I spread your legs again
And push way more than the head in
Inch by inch
Until my name on your lips
Sounds like sin
Yeah, what's my name, girl?
Uhn, say it again

On Tuesday, July 7th, the day after the city let
Ebenezer Baptist Church burn to the ground, Leo and Carla
made the front page again. The article was written by Cecil
Johnson, but the photo was not taken by him. It was the
picture Pastor Warren's daughter Nadine snapped while the
church was still up in flames.

In the picture, Leo held Carla with one arm and toted
his shotgun in the other hand. His expression was angry and
distraught, hers was focused and vigilant. In the

background, the devil's work was visible for all to see. Bright flames burst from the church's windows and licked the sky. Even though the lovers had yet to consummate their relationship at the time the picture was taken, their affection for one another was palpable. Anyone who read the paper that day could see it. Leo had seen many powerful photos during the Civil Rights Movement, and he ranked this picture among the best of them.

The bold headline above the photo read **ARSONIST BURNS NEGRO CHURCH**. Cecil's article was factual, but it was borderline editorial, as he gave a passionate depiction of the climate of hate in Overbrook Meadows. Despite it all, he wrote about beauty he saw on the horizon. He concluded the article with a direct quote from the speech Leo had given that morning:

"We will integrate those schools! The people attacking us have done nothing but bring us closer together!"

The following Sunday, a record number of 400 people attended church services at Ebenezer Baptist. True to his word, Pastor Warren gave the sermon from the front porch of his home, while the parishioners either sat or stood in the lawn. The pastor's voice boomed so loudly, he didn't need a microphone or megaphone.

After the service, everyone stayed to offer whatever help they could to Leo's campaign. They made more signs and flyers and offered more donations. The pastor, his wife and several deacons barbecued for the masses and provided a steady flow of lemonade to counter the afternoon heat. There were no protesters that day, but the police chief dispatched two squad cars, which were conspicuously parked at the bottom of the hill, just in case.

Leo and Carla were the last to leave the pastor's home that day. Even with several organizers helping them clean up and get all their supplies together, they were both exhausted. But the drive home highlighted the fruits of their labors. Leo saw his face or one of his campaign signs every few blocks. He and Carla were tickled pink. If the battle could be waged with visibility alone, victory was surely in their hands. But they understood visibility could only get them so far.

On Tuesday, September 8th, the good people of Overbrook Meadows went to the polls to vote for mayor and several city council seats. When the polls closed that evening, the race was too close to call. Leo was a ball of nerves that night. Carla pulled his hand away from his mouth, to stop him from biting his nails.

She told him, "If it's too close to call, that's a good thing. We can't do anything but wait for them to count the rest of the ballots. No point in stressing over it now. It's out of our hands."

Leo agreed with her, but that didn't stop his stomach from churning or alleviate his headache.

"Come on," Carla said, heading to his bedroom.

In the hallway she unzipped her skirt and pushed it down her hips. Leo's eyes widened at the sight of her panties, which were barely able to contain her luscious cheeks.

"I can help you get your mind off those votes," she said, before disappearing down the hallway.

Leo knew this was only a temporary fix, but his stomach instantly felt better. He sprang from his easy chair as if he heard a rattlesnake beneath it.

The next morning the city learned Mayor Holloway managed to hold on to his seat by less than 1,000 votes. Leo was devastated, but everyone agreed his ability to garnish so many votes and get the race so close was a major victory – especially considering he had no political experience and had announced his candidacy only two months ago. Surely Mayor Holloway was sweating in his boots last night.

The votes proved the people of Overbrook Meadows, well, almost half of them, were willing to go to unprecedented lengths to integrate the schools, even if it meant electing their first black mayor. Knowing the tide of segregation had changed, Mayor Holloway would have to act on it, or risk the wrath of his constituents.

Leo took solace in these words. His team made him feel better about losing, but there was nothing they could do to put a smile on his face. He retreated to his law office, hoping to decompress, but there was no respite there. Calls from well-wishers were incessant. Initially Leo instructed Ruby to take a message, but he eventually decided to accept the calls. After all they had done for him, the least he could do was thank them personally.

Overbrook Meadows did not close I.M. Terrell until 1971, a year after Leo's mayoral run. That summer, the school board prepared parents and students for the rollout of integration in the fall. When the schools reopened in September, the black students could finally attend the campuses closest to their homes.

There were a few angry glares in the white faces that dropped their children off for school that day, but there were no protests. Overbrook Meadows had no Ruby Bridges, Autherine Lucy or Little Rock Nine.

As expected, Mayor Holloway took full credit for bringing Overbrook Meadows into a beautiful new future with the peaceful integration.

A month later, on Sunday, October 15th, Leo and Carla met at the new and improved Ebenezer Baptist Church, which was located on the same spot as the building ravished by fire a few years ago. Although the old church was historic, with breaths of nostalgia at every turn, there was no disputing the new church was better. Built with all of the modern amenities and a much larger budget (thanks to a slew of donations from as far away as California and New York), Ebenezer was now the biggest church in the city.

The extra space was necessary, because the congregation boom Pastor Warren enjoyed during Leo's campaign never waned. In fact, the number of faithful parishioners who came to worship every weekend and Wednesday night continued to grow.

That Sunday, Pastor Warren preached dutifully to his usual crowd, but the after-church festivities was the bigger draw. At one p.m., Leo stood proudly before the pastor; looking extremely dapper in a new tuxedo, flanked by his four groomsmen. Across from them, Carla's bridesmaids were stunning in identical powder blue dresses.

But no one – not in the church, the city or the whole state of Texas – was more beautiful than the woman who appeared when the front doors of the church opened wide, flooding the aisle with bright sunlight and a glimpse of heaven. Leo's heart thumped sweetly as he watched his bride approach, arm in arm with her father.

The attendees gasped at the beauty of her dress. Rather than a traditional train, her veil flowed six feet behind her. Her ten-year-old niece carried it dutifully. The smile on Leo's face made it clear he was the luckiest man on earth. A lump formed in his throat as Carla's graceful steps brought her closer to becoming his wife until the end of time. If ever there was a vision so lovely, Leo would be hard-pressed to find it.

Although Carla was never one to let a little thing like *etiquette* dictate her choices, Leo was grateful the life growing inside her womb had not started to show. Of course there was sure to be a few prudes with raised eyebrows when their child was born. Hopefully not many people would take the time to do the math.

KEITH THOMAS WALKER

** I hope you enjoyed Leo and Carla's story. This is my first historical romance, and I had a lot of fun producing it. I'm sure you noticed the line between fact and fiction was not always clear in this book. Please continue reading to find out how much of this *fiction* story is actually *non-fiction*... **

FACT VS. FICTION

I've never written a historical romance, and I must say I truly enjoyed it. I find this interesting, because I hated history when I was in high school. Too many dates and names and locations. My classes always seemed to be set up for rote memorization, and I find that style of learning **boring**! But after graduation, most likely because I no longer had to memorize the things I read, history became very intriguing. I can study wars or The Civil Rights movement for hours and never get enough.

For this book, I had to do quite a bit of research, because I didn't want to misconstrue any of the facts I put forth. Overall this story is fiction, but there are so many real events intertwined, it may be hard to tell.

First of all, Leo and Carla are figments of my imagination. I know! Wouldn't it be cool if they actually existed? Likewise, Mayor Holloway, Councilman Mario Pratt, Pastor Jeremiah Warren, his church and family are all contrived by myself. With **a few notable exceptions**, all of the characters in this book are fictitious.

Now let's get to the real stuff! If you haven't caught on by reading my other books (or if you haven't read any of my other books – which hurts my feelings), Overbrook Meadows is a fictionalized version of **Fort Worth, Texas**. All of my books take place in this city. Fort Worth is my hometown, and it's a small way to pay homage.

Everything in this book about **I.M. Terrell** is true. It was the only high school for black students in Fort Worth all the way up until 1967. Students were bussed from as far away as Arlington, Burleson and Weatherford. Weatherford is 30 miles away. The school was initially named the East Ninth Street Colored School when it was first opened in 1882. It was the first free public school for blacks in Fort Worth. **Isaiah Milligan Terrell** was the school's principal. He later became the Superintendent of Colored Schools in 1890.

In 1906, the school moved to the intersection of East Twelfth and Steadman and was renamed North Side Colored School Number 11. It was renamed I.M. Terrell High School in 1921, in honor of its former principal. As you can imagine, the school suffered from lack of funding. In its early years, the building had no cafeteria, gym or library. There were not a lot of classrooms for teaching, and all of the textbooks were hand-me-downs from the white schools.

In 1938, the school moved once again to what was once a white elementary school in the Baptist Hill neighborhood. Yup, even our school building was a hand-me-down. By 1940, the school had 26 faculty members serving 900 high school students. The school was closed in 1973, when racial integration was finally implemented in Fort Worth's schools. It reopened in 1998 as I.M. Terrell Elementary School and is still standing today.

Unlike the strife depicted in this book, there is no documented civil unrest during the school integration phase of Fort Worth's history. Nothing I've read indicates the city faced protests when the schools were integrated in **1967** (rather than in **1971**, as *Election Day* indicates).

Although **Isaiah Milligan Terrell** wasn't a character in this book, I'd like to highlight some of his other accomplishments: In 1885, he and 12 other colleagues organized the Colored Teachers State Association of Texas. In 1915, he became the fifth principal of Prairie View State Normal and Industrial College. In 1918, he was named president of Houston College. In 1923, Terrell became superintendent of Union Hospital. In 1925 he secured funding for the Houston Negro Hospital. At its dedication in 1926, he was named the first superintendent.

The **Butler Housing Projects**, which is located directly behind I.M. Terrell, is real, and it is as economically disadvantaged as depicted in this story. The projects were constructed between 1939 and 1940 to remedy the tumbledown shacks where blacks once lived near the Trinity River (Trinity Bottoms). If not down by the river, poor blacks occupied other areas in the city that were considered undesirable by whites, like the Buttermilk Flats, Irish Town and Baptist Hill.

The Butler Projects were named after **Henry H. Butler**, who was an important figure in the black community. Unfortunately, I wasn't able to uncover much about him. Multiple websites mention him briefly, but the only information they provide is Butler was "an educator and Civil War veteran."

Although he didn't have a major role in this story, **Dr. Edward Guinn** is a true hometown hero. Guinn's parents moved to Fort Worth after the civil war, and he was raised in a prosperous neighborhood. After graduating from medical school, he trained in Pennsylvania hospitals before returning to Fort Worth. Dr. Guinn could've remained out of state or worked at one of our hospitals, but in 1958 he chose to open a practice in Stop Six, a poor, black community that was often referred to as a "hellhole."

Dr. Guinn had no political aspirations, but he answered the call when a group of black students from Texas Christian University encouraged him to run for a city council seat. Guinn lost the first time, but after currying favor with Amon Carter (a well-known Fort Worth philanthropist) and other members of the city's establishment, he easily won his second run for office.

During Dr. Guinn's term as a city council member, Fort Worth established EMS services, which replaced the funeral homes that once served as ambulances. The city avoided race riots that plagued other cities. While Guinn was on the city council, Fort Worth purchased land for the DFW airport. Dr. Guinn served on the state's Criminal Justice Panel, dined with LBJ at the White House, and greeted visiting dignitaries. He did all of this while still practicing medicine. As the only doctor in Stop Six, he considered himself "always on call."

There were plenty of calls for Dr. Guinn to run for higher office and move his clinic to a better neighborhood, but he never did either. After two terms, he retired from politics and returned to his medical practice. Dr. Guinn is **still** practicing medicine in Stop Six today. Yes, he's 93 years old and very much alive! (I guess you can tell how amazing I think he is!)

The last non-fiction character in this book is reporter **Cecil Johnson**. I wish I could tell you more about him, other than the fact that he was the first black reporter to work for the *Fort Worth Star Telegram* (*Overbrook Meadows Telegram* in this book). But I was unable to uncover additional biographical information. Personally, I think his accomplishment is worthy of a write-up *somewhere*, but at this time, history books have not dedicated a chapter to Mr. Johnson.

I did, however, uncover articles Cecil Johnson wrote, so I was able to align my character's beliefs with his. Interestingly, some of the research I did on the history of Fort Worth (and Dr. Guinn in particular) was traced back to an article written by Cecil Johnson.

The article I enjoyed the most is titled *Black, Liberal and Proud*. In this commentary, Mr. Johnson explains why he's, well, black, liberal and proud. I encourage you to research this reporter. I enjoy his writing style, and I'm sure you will too. If you happen to uncover more biographical information about him, I would love to hear about it. Contact me at keithwalkerbooks@yahoo.com.

Oh, and the information presented in this book about **White Settlement** is accurate as well. The city is located west of Fort Worth. There were once two settlements in the area, one being predominantly white and the other occupied by Native Americans. They named the first area "White Settlement" to distinguish it from the Native Americans.

This is clearly racist, and in 2005 city leaders attempted to rectify it. They proposed renaming the city "West Settlement" and put the vote to the people. With a vote of 2,388 to 219, the name change was overwhelming rejected. If this surprises you, it's probably because you ain't never been to White Settlement, partner!

This wraps up my *Fact vs. Fiction* section. I encourage you to check out the **school integration**

timeline I've included on the next few pages. Hopefully none of the information I've presented in the previous pages is inaccurate, but if you come across something that is, don't hesitate to notify me. I can upload changes to an eBook in 48 hours. Correcting an error in the paperback version is a bit more difficult, but if it needs to be done, I won't hesitate to do the right thing.

I live to learn.

SCHOOL INTEGRATION TIMELINE

1849 The Massachusetts Supreme Court rules that segregated schools are permissible under the state's constitution. *(Roberts v. City of Boston)* The U.S. Supreme Court will later use this case to support the "separate but equal" doctrine.

1857 With the *Dred Scott* decision, the Supreme Court upholds the denial of citizenship to African Americans and rules that descendants of slaves are "so far inferior that they had no rights which the white man was bound to respect."

1861 Southern states secede from the Union. The Civil War begins.

1863 President Lincoln issues the Emancipation Proclamation, freeing slaves in Southern states. Because the Civil War is ongoing, the Proclamation has little practical effect.

1865 The Civil War ends. The Thirteenth Amendment is enacted to abolish slavery.

1868 The Fourteenth Amendment is ratified, guaranteeing "equal protection under the law," which extends citizenship to African Americans.

1875 Congress passes the Civil Rights Act of 1875, which bans racial discrimination in public accommodations.

1883 The Supreme Court strikes down the Civil Rights Act of 1875 finding that discrimination by individuals or private businesses is constitutional.

1890 Louisiana passes the first Jim Crow law requiring separate accommodations for Whites and Blacks.

1896 The Supreme Court authorizes segregation in *Plessy v. Ferguson,* finding Louisiana's "separate but equal" law constitutional. The ruling, built on notions of white supremacy and black inferiority, provides legal justification for Jim Crow laws in southern states.

1899 The Supreme Court allows a state to levy taxes on black and white citizens alike while providing a public school for white children only. *(Cumming v. Richmond (Ga.) County Board of Education)*

1908 The Supreme Court upholds a state's authority to require a private college to operate on a segregated basis despite the wishes of the school. *(Berea College v. Kentucky)*

1927 The Supreme Court finds that states possess the right to define a Chinese student as non-white for the purpose of segregating public schools. *(Gong Lum v. Rice)*

1936 The Maryland Supreme Court orders the state's white law school to enroll a black student because there is no state-supported law school for Blacks in Maryland. *(University of Maryland v. Murray)*

1938 The Supreme Court rules the practice of sending black students out of state for legal training when the state provides a law school for whites within its borders does not fulfill the state's "separate but equal" obligation. The Court orders Missouri's all-white law school to grant admission to an African American student. *(Missouri ex rel. Gaines v. Canada)*

1940 A federal court requires equal salaries for African American and white teachers. *(Alston v. School Board of City of Norfolk)*

1947 In a precursor to the *Brown* case, a federal appeals court strikes down segregated schooling for Mexican American and white students. *(Westminster School Dist. v. Mendez)* The verdict prompts California Governor Earl Warren to repeal a state law calling for segregation of Native American and Asian American students.

1948 Arkansas desegregates its state university.
The Supreme Court orders the admission of a black student to the University of Oklahoma School of Law, a white

school, because there is no law school for Blacks. *(Sipuel v. Board of Regents of the University of Oklahoma)*

1950 The Supreme Court rejects Texas' plan to create a new law school for black students rather than admit an African American to the state's whites-only law school. *(Sweatt v. Painter)*

The Supreme Court rules that learning in law school "cannot be effective in isolation from the individuals and institutions with which the law interacts." The decision stops short of overturning *Plessy*.

The Supreme Court holds that the policy of isolating a black student from his peers within a white law school is unconstitutional. *(McLaurin v. Oklahoma State Regents for Higher Education)*

Barbara Johns, a 16-year-old junior at Robert R. Moton High School in Farmville, Va., organizes and leads 450 students in an anti-school segregation strike.

1952 The Supreme Court hears oral arguments in *Brown v. Board of Education*. Thurgood Marshall, who will later become the first African American justice on the Supreme Court, is the lead counsel for the black school children.

1953 Earl Warren is appointed Chief Justice of the Supreme Court.

The Supreme Court hears the second round of arguments in *Brown v. Board of Education of Topeka*.

1954 In a unanimous opinion, the Supreme Court in *Brown v. Board of Education* overturns *Plessy* and declares that separate schools are "inherently unequal." The Court delays deciding on how to implement the decision and asks for another round of arguments.

The Court rules that the federal government is under the same duty as the states and must desegregate the Washington, D.C. schools. *(Bolling v. Sharpe)*

1955 In *Brown II,* the Supreme Court orders the lower federal courts to require desegregation "with all deliberate speed."

1955 Between 1955 and 1960, federal judges will hold more than 200 school desegregation hearings.

1956 Tennessee Governor Frank Clement calls in the National Guard after white mobs attempt to block the desegregation of a high school.

Under court order, the University of Alabama admits Autherine Lucy, its first African American student. White students and residents riot. Lucy is suspended and later expelled for criticizing the university.

The Virginia legislature calls for "massive resistance" to school desegregation and pledges to close schools under desegregation orders.

1957 More than 1,000 paratroopers from the 101st Airborne Division and a federalized Arkansas National Guard protect nine black students integrating Central High School in Little Rock, Ark.

1958 The Supreme Court rules that fear of social unrest or violence, whether real or constructed by those wishing to oppose integration, does not excuse state governments from complying with *Brown. (Cooper v. Aaron)*

10,000 young people march in Washington, D.C., in support of integration.

1959 25,000 young people march in Washington, D.C., in support of integration.

Prince Edward County, Va., officials close their public schools rather than integrate them. White students attend private academies; black students do not head back to class until 1963, when the Ford Foundation funds private black schools. The Supreme Court orders the county to reopen its schools on a desegregated basis in 1964.

1960 In New Orleans, federal marshals shielded Ruby Bridges, Gail St. Etienne, Leona Tate and Tessie Prevost from angry crowds as they enrolled in school.

1961 A federal district court orders the University of Georgia to admit African American students Hamilton Holmes and Charlayne Hunter. After a riot on campus, the two are suspended. A court later reinstates them.

1962 A federal appeals court orders the University of Mississippi to admit James Meredith, an African American student. Upon his arrival, a mob of more than 2,000 white people riots.

1963 Two African American students, Vivian Malone and James A. Hood, successfully register at the University of Alabama despite George Wallace's "stand in the schoolhouse door" — but only after President Kennedy federalizes the Alabama National Guard.

For the first time, a small number of black students in Alabama, Louisiana and Mississippi attend public elementary and secondary schools with white students.

1964 The Civil Rights Act of 1964 is adopted. Title IV of the Act authorizes the federal government to file school desegregation cases. Title VI of the Act prohibits discrimination in programs and activities, including schools, receiving federal financial assistance.

The Rev. Bruce Klunder is killed protesting the construction of a new segregated school in Cleveland, Ohio.

1968 The Supreme Court orders states to dismantle segregated school systems "root and branch." The Court identifies five factors — facilities, staff, faculty, extracurricular activities and transportation — to be used to gauge a school system's compliance with the mandate of *Brown. (Green v. County School Board of New Kent County)*

In a private note to Justice Brennan, Justice Warren writes: "When this opinion is handed down, the traffic light will have changed from *Brown* to *Green*. Amen!"

1969 The Supreme Court declares the "all deliberate speed" standard is no longer constitutionally permissible and orders the immediate desegregation of Mississippi schools. *(Alexander v. Holmes County Board of Education)*

1971 The Court approves busing, magnet schools, compensatory education and other tools as appropriate remedies to overcome the role of residential segregation in perpetuating racially segregated schools. *(Swann v. Charlotte-Mecklenberg Board of Education)*

1972 The Supreme Court refuses to allow public school systems to avoid desegregation by creating new, mostly or all-white "splinter districts." *(Wright v. Council of the City of Emporia; United States v. Scotland Neck City Board of Education)*

Brown's legacy extends to gender. Title IX of the Educational Amendments of 1972 is passed prohibiting sex discrimination in any educational program that receives federal financial assistance.

1973 Section 504 of the Rehabilitation Act is passed prohibiting schools from discriminating against students with mental or physical impairments.

The Supreme Court rules that states cannot provide textbooks to racially segregated private schools to avoid integration mandates. *(Norwood v. Harrison)*

The Supreme Court finds that the Denver school board intentionally segregated Mexican American and black students from white students. *(Keyes v. Denver School District No. 1)* The Court distinguishes between state-mandated segregation *(de jure)* and segregation that is the result of private choices *(de facto)*. The latter form of segregation, the Court rules, is not unconstitutional.

The Supreme Court rules that education is not a "fundamental right" and that the Constitution does not require equal education expenditures within a state. *(San Antonio Independent School District v. Rodriguez)* The ruling has the effect of locking minority and poor children who live in low-income areas into inferior schools.

1974 The Supreme Court blocks metropolitan-wide desegregation plans as a means to desegregate urban schools with high minority populations. *(Milliken v. Bradley)* As a result, *Brown* will not have a substantial impact on many racially isolated urban districts.

Non-English-speaking Chinese students file suit against the San Francisco Unified School District for failing to provide instruction to those with limited English proficiency. The Supreme Court rules that the failure to do so violates Title VI's prohibition of national origin, race or color discrimination in school districts receiving federal funds. *(Lau v. Nichols)*

1978 A fractured Supreme Court declares the affirmative action admissions program for the University of California Davis Medical School unconstitutional because it set aside a specific number of seats for black and Latino students. The Court rules that race can be a factor in university admissions, but it cannot be the deciding factor. *(Regents of the University of California v. Bakke)*

1982 The Supreme Court rejects tax exemptions for private religious schools that discriminate. *(Bob Jones University v. U.S.; Goldboro Christian Schools v. U.S.)*

1986 For the first time, a federal court finds that once a school district meets the *Green* factors, it can be released from its desegregation plan and returned to local control. *(Riddick v. School Board of the City of Norfolk, Virginia)*

1988 School integration reaches its all-time high; almost 45% of black students in the United States are attending majority-white schools.

1991 Emphasizing that court orders are not intended "to operate in perpetuity," the Supreme Court makes it easier for formerly segregated school systems to fulfill their obligations under desegregation decrees. *(Board of Education of Oklahoma City v. Dowell)* After being released from a court order, the Oklahoma City school system abandons its desegregation efforts and returns to neighborhood schools.

1992 The Supreme Court further speeds the end of desegregation cases, ruling that school systems can fulfill their obligations in an incremental fashion. *(Freeman v. Pitts)*

The Supreme Court rules that the adoption of race-neutral measures does not, by itself, fulfill the Constitutional obligation to desegregate colleges and universities that were segregated by law. *(United States v. Fordice)*

1995 The Supreme Court sets a new goal for desegregation plans: the return of schools to local control. It emphasizes again that judicial remedies were intended to be "limited in time and extent." *(Missouri v. Jenkins)*

1996 A federal appeals court prohibits the use of race in college and university admissions, ending affirmative action in Louisiana, Texas and Mississippi. *(Hopwood v. Texas)*

2001 White parents in Charlotte, N.C., schools successfully seek an end to the desegregation process and a bar to the use of race in making student assignments.

2002 A report from Harvard's Civil Rights Project concludes that America's schools are resegregating.

2003 The Supreme Court upholds diversity as a rationale for affirmative action programs in higher education admissions but concludes that point systems are not appropriate. *(Grutter v. Bollinger; Gratz v. Bollinger)*
    A federal district court case affirms the value of racial diversity and race-conscious student assignment plans in K-12 education. *(Lynn v. Comfort)*
    A study by Harvard's Civil Rights Project finds that schools were more segregated in 2000 than in 1970 when busing for desegregation began.

2004 The nation marks the 50th anniversary of *Brown v. Board of Education.*

2007 In *Parents Involved,* the Supreme Court finds voluntary school integration plans unconstitutional, paving the way for contemporary school segregation to escalate.

Next Decades novel coming September 1ˢᵗ

Layla Johnson had a picture perfect life: a career as an educator, a beautiful daughter, a son on the way, and a loving husband. Only Layla didn't count on the effect the burgeoning war on drugs would have on her family and her world. And on one rainy night, everything that she worked to attain is destroyed. Now, she's on her own, with two young children, a mounting pile of debt...and the past knocking at her door.

Lincoln Wilson broke the one thing he treasured most. Instead of spending the rest of his life doting on his beautiful wife and children, he's alone, haunted by his many mistakes. Determined to make amends, Lincoln works to put the pieces of his life back together again. And although it's an uphill battle, he is up for the challenge. The last step in Lincoln's program is to prove to his wife that he can be the man she needs. When he shows up on her doorstep ready to reclaim his life, will Layla let him in?

Please continue reading the first
two chapters of *Brick House*...

CHAPTER ONE
THE MORNING AFTER
(BRICK HOUSE)

The morning after.
Ugh.
Korah's nostrils flared as the delectable aroma of biscuits and sausage and possibly hash browns made it all the way from the kitchen to her large, sundrenched bedroom on the second floor. She frowned rather than smile at the thought of a man cooking for her. She did not look forward to the conversation she and Quincy would have when she went downstairs to greet him.

She rolled over and squinted at the alarm clock on her nightstand. It was 7:22 am. She should've been up and amongst the working world by now, or at least in the midst of the morning commuters. She rolled back over to her other side, thankful that she didn't have a headache. All things considered, she felt pretty good – which was not usually the case when she drank as much as she did last night.

She wondered how Quincy managed to weasel his way into her home and her bedroom in the wee hours of the morning, but of course she knew. It all started with her tight red dress that ran out of material midway down her thighs and the look of utter foolishness Quincy wore when she answered the door for him and he ran his wolf eyes up and down her curvy frame.

Yesterday was his birthday. Korah and Quincy had been broken up for months, but they remained cordial. So she wasn't opposed to accompanying him to the Red Flamingo for a big party he and his friends planned. Last night Quincy looked surprisingly dapper in a new Armani suit, and Korah complemented him as the perfect arm candy. Her hair was down and flowing. Her legs were long, her dark cleavage plentiful. She garnished just as much attention as the birthday boy, much to her and Quincy's delight.

They were having so much fun, she didn't protest when Quincy began holding her hand when he introduced her around the room. As the night progressed, he kept an arm possessively around her waist as they strolled the lively locale, and Korah didn't put a stop to that either.

She should have, but she didn't.

The alcohol no doubt played a big part in it. The Red Flamingo Club had a signature drink called "*Paradise*." It was pink in color and sweet to the taste and loaded with vodka, gin and rum. Korah was sufficiently buzzed after her second one. But Quincy kept ordering them, and she kept drinking. It was a party, after all.

As the clock struck midnight, and the party kicked into second gear, Korah and her ex-boyfriend tripped the light fantastic. She wasn't the best dancer, but she was better than Quincy and most of the other women who hit the dance floor that night. Quincy was absolutely gushing with appreciation for her accompanying him. And Korah had to admit she was having a lot of fun as well.

They grinded under the strobe lights like lovers, and at some point Korah stopped shooing his hands away when they slipped from her waist to her hips down to her swollen derriere. She kept her arms around Quincy's neck and stared into his eager, hungry eyes. Korah's brown orbs were low and intoxicated. Her lips were full and moist. Quincy's skin was dark and smooth like polished mahogany. He pulled her hips very close to his, and he hummed in her ear when Korah didn't protest that either.

She felt how hard and how badly he wanted her. She knew she shouldn't dip her toes in those forbidden waters, but sometimes (if there's enough time passed and alcohol involved) familiarity wins out over good judgment.

When Quincy drove her home in his sleek Mercedes E-Class, it was nearly two am, and his hormones had been raging for hours. He didn't attempt a pickup line when he killed the engine. He simply leaned over the center console for the kiss he'd been yearning for, and Korah met him halfway. His tongue slipped into her mouth immediately. Spurred on by the unexpected green light, his hand boldly moved from his lap to hers, in search of the blazing heat between her legs. He rubbed the outside of her panties with long, skillful fingers, and then he slipped her panties to the side.

He grunted when he encountered her incredible moistness, and he commenced to finger her while they made out like teenagers.

Korah thought his tongue tasted like Paradise. She sucked his lips and bucked her hips against his hand. She rode his stiff fingers until her chest was moist with sweat and the volume of her moans drowned out Ralph Tresvant, who was crooning on an oldies R&B station.

Though I love the girl, I know that the best thing is for us to be apart...

Korah's breathing became heavier and heavier, until her orgasm thundered like cannon fire, leaving her squealing and numb and tingly all over.

She still didn't agree with her choice of partners for the night, but as she shielded her face from the sunlight the next morning, she couldn't help but smile at the memory.

By the time she and Quincy made it inside her home, his dick pitched a mighty tent in his slacks. Korah was sufficiently plastered, but did have sense enough to make him return to his car to get a condom. Aside from that, she let Quincy have her any way he wanted to. He came too quickly, as was his tradition, but he made up for it when Korah rolled him onto his back and straddled his face.

Oooh.

That memory made Korah moan aloud and squeeze her legs together as a sweet aftershock rolled up her thighs and made her clit swell pleasantly. She grinned as she pulled her sheets up over her shoulders, content to traipse down memory lane a while longer.

By the time Quincy got hard again, his mouth and cheeks were slick and glistening with Korah's essence. She looked down at him with both hands gripping the top of the headboard, thinking he was such a sloppy eater. Quincy grinned up at her and then moved to a more dominant position behind her.

Korah appreciated his enthusiasm, but by then she was exhausted, nearly to the point of passing out. Quincy grabbed hold of her thighs and hiked her hips up as she lowered her face onto her pillows. Quincy wasn't necessarily *packing*, but he knew how to work with what he had. He never filled her completely, but he maximized his movements, ensuring his dick provided constant stimulus to her clitoris with each stroke.

It was around this time that Korah began to contemplate the folly of her actions. She and Quincy were not in a relationship anymore. He had courted her for four months, and it took approximately that long for Korah to decide they were already in a rut. It wasn't Quincy's fault. He was hardworking and successful and cultured. But Korah longed for something *different.*

Something exciting.

She didn't need him to be a mafia hit man, but Quincy's boring life as an accountant didn't fit the bill, either.

Unfortunately, like a few other men Korah dumped in her lifetime, Quincy was forever hopeful that they could reignite the fires that once kept their love blazing. He would no doubt think he was working his way back into her life as he worked his dick between her hot, wet walls – and that was a problem.

Any hopes that he would understand (as Korah did) that this was a one-time thing were dashed when she awakened to an empty bed and the smell of biscuits and sausage and possibly hash browns wafting from her kitchen. She knew Quincy was preparing the meal with a fool-hearty smile pasted on his face, and she knew he'd paint her out to be a bitch when she went down there to burst his bubble.

Ugh.

Korah sighed, her smile completely gone now. She threw back the sheets and sat up in bed. She was completely nude. Her slight movement brought with it the first throbs of a mild headache.

Her bedroom was big and beautiful – not nearly as disheveled as she thought it would be. Her dress was on the floor in the doorway. Her bra was a few feet away from it. She only saw one of her heels, and she had no idea where her panties were. Knowing Quincy, they were probably balled-up in his pocket, which was another good reason to put him and his birthday bash behind her.

She checked the clock again. It was 7:30 now. Korah rose to her feet and stopped by the bathroom to grab a robe before she went downstairs. She found Quincy in the kitchen putting the finishing touches on her breakfast plate. In addition to the biscuits and sausage, he made her eggs and split a grapefruit in half. Korah didn't see the other half of the grapefruit anywhere. She hoped that meant he had already eaten, because she didn't want him to leave upset *and* hungry.

Quincy was barefoot, but he wore his slacks and tee shirt from last night. He was of average height and build.

He sported a short afro that Korah wasn't particularly fond of, but she did like his smooth, dark skin and the way he kept his moustache and beard trimmed perfectly. He turned and smiled when he heard her bare feet on the tiles behind him. He turned the stove off and placed his spatula on the counter before he approached her.

He wrapped his arms around her waist and held her tightly, like they were newlyweds. Korah grimaced as he nuzzled his face against her neck. She didn't mind his affection, just as she didn't mind the pleasure he provided last night. But it was never easy with this man. A simple smile could take his heart on a journey.

He backed away and frowned when he noticed her expression.

"Good morning. What's wrong?"

"Nothing," Korah said. "You been up for a while?"

"Yeah." Quincy turned and hefted her plate. "I made you breakfast." He presented to her as if she was a sex goddess, and it was an offering.

Korah didn't care for greasy foods first thing in the morning, but she didn't want to be rude. She plucked one of the small sausage links from the plate and ate it. She even managed to smile.

"Thank you very much. Don't you have to be at work this morning?"

"I called them," Quincy said. "It's okay if I'm a little late."

"Hmmm. Not me," Korah said. She tied her robe straps together and stretched lazily. "I gotta get a move on."

"Oh, that's okay," Quincy said. He smiled. "Thanks again for coming to my party. You looked so good last night. You look good now, too."

"Thank you," Korah said. "But I know I look like crap."

"Hell no you don't," Quincy said. "Even in your robe, you look better than most of the women I see on a daily basis."

At five foot, eight inches, Korah was roughly the same height as Quincy. And like him, she had rich skin, like coffee with just a hint of cream. Even the fluffy robe wasn't enough to hide her curves, which Korah had to admit were pleasing to the eye.

At 46 years of age, her breasts weren't as perky as they once were, but they were nice and round, and even a cheap bra gave her mountains of cleavage. Her hips were spread enticingly, and her ass was soft and round. Korah's natural hair was shoulder-length. Her cheeks had sexy dimples that she didn't fully appreciate until she became an adult.

She told her ex-boyfriend, "I'm about to jump in the shower. Are you gonna leave before I get out, because I wanna lock the door."

"I don't have to," Quincy said with a dopey grin that reinforced Korah's thinking that he was about to get his feelings hurt. "I can jump in the shower with you, if you don't mind..."

"You can use the shower down here," Korah offered. "I'm already running late. I don't need any of your *distractions*." She smiled, hoping to soften the blow.

Quincy smiled too. "Alright. I get it. Last night is over, and you're ready to get back to your regularly scheduled life."

Korah raised an eyebrow, thinking he wasn't as lovesick as she thought. "Yeah. That's what I want."

"Okay," Quincy said. He removed his cellphone from his pocket and accessed the calendar app. "I was wondering if you wanted to catch a dinner at the new steakhouse that opened downtown. I'm busy for the rest of the week, but—"

"No, I don't think that's a good idea," Korah said, stopping his thumb in mid-swipe.

He looked up at her. "Oh. Um, why not?"

Korah rolled her eyes inwardly. "Because we're not together anymore, Quincy. We broke up two months ago. We shouldn't go on dates."

His smile fell. "Yeah, but, last night..."

"I know," Korah said with a sigh. "I knew it was probably gonna be trouble, but I–"

"There's no trouble," Quincy interjected, shaking his head. "I had a good time. I thought you did, too."

"I did," Korah said. She smiled. "I had a great time with you last night."

"But you're saying it's over?"

"Well, yeah," she said. "Today's a new day. I gotta get to work."

"I'm talking about us."

Korah brought a hand to her face and rubbed her eye sockets. "Quincy, you know we're not together anymore. You asked me to be your date for your party, and I said I would. I drank a lot more than I should have, and–"

"So that was all about you drinking? Now you wanna blame it on the alcohol?"

"Quincy, I don't have to blame it on anything. We're both grown. I didn't say I was drunk. I'm just saying I drank more than I should've, and I didn't think things through."

"So you are saying you wouldn't have slept with me, if you were sober..."

Korah shook her head in exasperation. "Quincy, sleeping with you is not the problem. What's happening right now is the problem. We had a good time last night, and you're about to ruin it by–"

"I'm ruining it?"

"Yes, you're making this very awkward," Korah confirmed.

Quincy returned his phone to his pocket and folded his arms over his chest. "Well excuse me for thinking that when two people kiss and hold hands and make love it probably means they're in a relationship."

"It was your birthday," she said. "We had a good time. No need to end it on a sour note."

"So it meant nothing to you. That's what you're saying, right?"

Anger was getting the best of him, but Korah was undeterred. His temper was another reason she broke up with him in the first place. And she couldn't stand his clinginess. Quincy didn't realize that putting both of these characteristics on display this morning only bolstered her negative feelings about him and made her feel less like a heartless bitch for hurting his feelings.

"It certainly didn't mean we were getting back together," she said plainly. "Now, if you want to shower before you go–"

"You're acting like a real *bitch*," Quincy decided.

Korah grinned. She knew that would be the end result, no matter how she tried to schmooze this little talk.

"And you think it's funny," he spat.

"No, Quincy. I think you're acting really immature right now. And I'm thinking this will be the last time I agree to go *anywhere* with your crazy ass. We shouldn't have slept together. I get it. Now could you please leave, so I can get ready for work?"

All of his resolve dissipated right before her eyes. "I'm sorry, Korah. I didn't mean to get upset. You're right. I read too much into it. I don't wanna leave here on bad terms."

Too late for that.

"Okay," she said. "It's fine. So did you wanna take a shower before you go, or..."

"Um, no," he said "I know you're in a rush. I'll just grab my things and stop by my place on the way to work. I gotta get some clean clothes anyway."

"Okay," Korah said.

She waited in the living room while he gathered his shoes, shirt and jacket from the bedroom. He approached her a few minutes later, fully dressed and hoping to make amends, but Korah was sick of his stupid face by then. She clenched her teeth when he gave her a kiss on the cheek on his way out.

When did booty calls get so complicated? she wondered as she locked the door behind him. *I'm getting too old for this.* But that didn't seem right, either. Korah still felt young enough to take the world by storm.

She decided Quincy was the one at fault when she stepped into the shower. By the time she got out, she was able to put the whole silly incident behind her – except for her orgasms. She didn't know when she'd reach that level of contentment again, so she held on to the memories of their lovemaking for a little while longer.

When she finally got dressed for work, it was after eight, and Korah had to return three business calls she'd missed. Her son Devin seemed to have the most significant issues, so when she rolled out of her driveway, Korah pointed her Pathfinder in his direction.

Devin Jr. served as foreman for the construction company Korah added to the family business four years ago. Prior to that, Texas Builders functioned only as a general contractor. They had to hire a construction team to work the sites Korah won bids on.

Establishing their own construction company increased profits dramatically. Not only was her squad guaranteed to work their properties, but Korah also sent them to work for other contractors who still had to outsource their manual labor.

The date was Monday, September 8th. The weather in Overbrook Meadows was warm and cloudy, but not too humid that morning. The cloud cover was expected to blow over by noon, leaving ideal conditions for Devin's 30-man crew. Today they were erecting a 7-11 at the corner of Hemphill and Sycamore School Road.

The worksite was bustling with activity when Korah arrived at the property, but she had no problem spotting her son. At six-foot-four inches tall, Devin stood head and shoulders above most of his employees. He was fair-skinned, like his father, and he had long arms and broad shoulders that made him a force to be reckoned with when he played ball in high school and college.

Devin Jr. could've taken his hoop dreams further if he gave it his all, but working for the family business had been his only dream, ever since he was constructing mini-malls out of Lego building blocks when he was in grade school. His father's death reinforced this legacy thirteen years ago, despite Korah's assurances that Devin Jr. was free to be whatever he wanted to be.

Seeing him now, Korah knew that she never really had a say in the matter. Her son was born to build things, just like his dad. At only 26 years of age, Devin Jr. was already fully in charge of multi-million dollar projects and was completely comfortable with the role. He was well-respected by his crew. And even though some of the business owners who hired them seemed unsure of the youngster when they first met him, by the end of the job they were always impressed and appreciative of Devin's work. In many cases, they were genuinely awed.

Korah parked her Navigator next to a large sign that read:

TEXAS BUILDERS
General Contractors
Construction
Renovations
555-225-6623

There were identical signs currently planted at six different construction sites throughout the city. Korah's chest swelled with pride, no matter how often she saw them.

She stepped out of her SUV wearing jeans with a tee-shirt that had their company logo printed prominently on the front and back. Korah snatched her hardhat from the backseat and pushed it down on her head before she stepped into the construction zone. She wore steel-toed boots, rather than pumps, but she still looked very feminine on the male-dominated property, despite the fact that she wore no makeup at all.

All of the construction workers knew that Korah was their boss' boss (and mother), and they were very respectful and quick to acknowledge her presence as she approached.

"Morning, Ms. Stewart!"

"Great to see you today!"

Korah smiled and nodded at their pleasantries. "Morning, boys. Gonna be a great day today."

"Yes Ma'am! Everything's coming along just fine."

Korah's smile faded when she reached her son, because Devin was not in a good mood at all. He briefly made eye-contact with her before he turned away slightly and continued yelling at whoever was on the other end of his cellphone.

"Who the hell told him to go down 35? What the hell do y'all do, just plug it in your GPS and take the shortest route? Everybody knows 35 is jacked up this time of morning. He could've hit 820 and been here by now!"

After a pause, Devin said, "That's not my fuc—" He caught himself and turned away from his mother even more. "That's not my fucking problem," he grumbled. "I got my concrete crew out here *right now*. Every minute your guy is late is costing me money! And if that batch is no good by the time it gets here, we're gonna have some serious problems..."

As she waited, Korah marveled at how much her son looked like his father. Devin kept his hair cut short, and he wore no moustache or goatee. The major difference between him and Devin Sr. was his irritability, but Korah didn't fault her son for that. His way of getting things done had proven successful time and time again.

Some bosses earned their employees' respect with perks and bonuses. Others preferred intimidation tactics. Devin Sr. built the company from the ground up without every raising his voice. Devin Jr. chose a different path.

When he got off the phone, he turned and gave his mother a brief hug.

"Hey, Mama. Sorry about that."

"What's wrong?"

"Concrete truck is stuck in traffic," Devin reported. "He added water to the mix twice already. The consistency will probably be all messed up by the time he gets here. And I got a crew of guys just *waiting*. It'll take another hour, if they have to get a new batch."

Korah turned and saw a group of strangers milling around the front of the store. They were all Hispanic, with brown, sun-beaten skin and work clothes that already looked soiled.

"I thought you had some concrete guys on your crew," Korah said, not happy that they had to look elsewhere for a portion of the labor.

"Everybody's tied up today," Devin said. "I wanna knock this parking lot out as soon as possible. This crew can get it done, if we ever get the damn concrete."

Korah saw that the foundation and rebar had already been laid perfectly. All they needed was the wet stuff.

"How many trucks are coming?"

Devin gave her a look. Korah caught herself and grinned. She knew he hated it when she got too deeply involved in his construction work. As a contractor, her role was to hire a construction company and let them do the job. She wouldn't normally poke her nose into their business unless there was a major problem. But it was hard to back off, since the construction crew was run by her baby, and it was part of her overall brand.

"So what you're telling me is we don't have a problem..."

Devin nodded and smiled brightly. "That's right, Mama. We do *not* have a problem."

Korah narrowed her eyes. Back when she used to outsource for construction, some of the foremen she hired would tell her the same thing when there was indeed *plenty* to worry about. As a rule, construction companies never want contractors to know how bad things really are.

"Alright," Korah said. "You hungry? You eat breakfast today?"

Devin patted his flat belly, still smiling. "Yes Ma'am. I ate a big breakfast. I'm full of energy."

His smile made Korah want to pinch his cheeks, but of course she would never do that. Not in public, anyway.

"When are you getting the windows installed?" she asked instead.

The store was nearly complete, with all four walls and the roof erected.

"As soon as we get the concrete work finished," Devin said. "The glass man should be here any minute. The electricians are coming today, too."

"You're doing a great job," she told him. "Have I told you how proud I am of you?"

"Yes, but you can say it again, if you wanna."

The boy would never know how much he meant to his mother. Korah loved him so much, it made her heart sigh.

"I'm very proud of you," she said. "But if that concrete doesn't get here in the next thirty minutes—"

"Mama, you—"

She held a finger up to silence him when her cellphone rang. Korah fully expected to see Quincy's number on the Caller ID, but the call came from her main office.

"Hey, what's up?"

"Good morning, Korah."

It was Priscilla, vice president of Texas Builders. The sound of her sweet voice put a genuine smile on Korah's face. Priscilla was 65 years old. She had been with the company since Korah's husband founded it in 1989. That was twenty-five years ago. Priscilla had been mentioning retirement for the past couple of years. Korah did not look forward to the inevitable day they would lose her expertise.

"Ms. Priscilla. Good morning! How are things?"

"Great!" Priscilla said. "Got good news about the bid."

Texas Builders had a dozen or more bids being considered at any given time, but Korah had no doubt as to which one Priscilla was referring to. This was The Big One: A new high school for Overbrook Meadows school district. The winner of the bid would be contracted to complete what would be the biggest project in the history of Korah's company. The school district had already set aside fifteen million dollars for the development. That kind of money made Korah's heart flutter.

Texas Builders had done well for themselves over the years, constructing churches, convenience stores and even a shopping center and a few small Walmarts. But the school district contract would take them to another level – especially since the contractor with the winning bid would also get first crack at other work in the district, which already included a new middle school and countless renovations.

This was the kind of job Devin Senior dreamed about many years ago, when all he had was a pocket full of ambition and a head full of dreams.

"What's the good news?" Korah asked, her heart light in her chest.

"We're in the top two," Priscilla announced. "We actually have a good chance of winning this thing."

Korah's face flushed with heat. She couldn't hide her elation. Even Devin Jr. loosened up when he saw the smile on her face.

"Are you coming to the office?" Priscilla asked.

"Yeah, I'm on my way."

"See you soon," Priscilla said and disconnected.

Korah regained her professional demeanor when she put her phone away. "I'll be back later," she told Devin. "I gotta check on a few things."

"What's going on?" her son asked, following her to her truck.

They both wore the same jeans and Texas Builders tees, but Devin was nearly a foot taller than his mom, and his shirt stretched nicely over his broad shoulders and prominent pectorals. His tool belt hung on his hips like a gunslinger. It was well-worn, sunburned leather, but it was still beautiful. It once belonged to his father.

"What are you so happy about?" he asked.

Korah looked back at him, her eyes glistening under the bib of her hardhat. "I think we might get the school," she told him.

"Oh yeah?" Devin's chest swelled with hope as well.

"You think you could build a school?" Korah teased as she opened her car door.

Devin offered his hand and helped her up into the cab of the truck, although it wasn't necessary. Korah placed her hardhat on the passenger seat and brushed her hair down with long, slender fingers.

"I reckon we can build one just as good as any of the others," Devin said, his big hands resting on the open window frame. "When will they make an announcement?"

"In about three weeks," Korah said.

He frowned. "I ain't got time to be anxious for that long," Devin said, backing away from her truck. "Got too much to do." But the delight in his eyes said otherwise.

"Well, get to it then," Korah said. She started her car and winked at him as she threw it in gear.

195

CHAPTER TWO
TEXAS BUILDERS
(BRICK HOUSE)

Korah met Devin Stewart Sr. during her junior year at Finley High, nearly three decades ago. Devin was a recent transfer from west Texas, and he was the talk of the school within a week of his arrival. All of the girls were attracted to his rugged, country boy looks, and many of the jocks hoped Devin's height and brown skin would translate to a new weapon on the basketball court or football field.

Much to their disappointment, Devin wasn't into organized sports. He participated enough to pass gym, but it was shop class that made his heart go pitty-pat. He and Korah were paired together for the menial task of building a birdhouse, but no construction assignment was menial for Devin.

Two weeks later they turned in a triple-decker monstrosity that was big enough to house a murder of crows. Korah had done little more than paint their birdhouse (she went with pink, against Devin's protests), but that was enough to garnish her a 100 for the assignment and an A for the course overall.

Korah and Devin didn't spend much side-by-side time working on the birdhouse, but they did see each other often enough to create a sense of intrigue on both sides. Korah wanted to know more about the first boy she ever met who took shop class so seriously, and Devin was smitten with Korah from the moment the teacher assigned her as his partner. Korah was tall and pretty with a bright smile and pink lip gloss that smelled like bubblegum. But she wasn't an airhead, like most of the other gorgeous girls at the school.

Devin was so nervous around her, it took him nearly a month to ask if she wanted to have lunch with him one day. The cafeteria served casserole and cornbread that afternoon. Devin couldn't eat one bite while sitting with Korah, which she thought was the cutest thing ever.

They were officially a couple throughout their senior year of high school, and many of Korah's fondest memories could be traced back to those magical times. Devin bought her the biggest, most beautiful mum for Finley's homecoming game that year, and he looked very debonair in the tuxedo he rented for their senior prom. Korah lost her virginity to Devin that night, and after graduation she began dreaming of the life they would one day share together.

Korah and Devin began college together at Texas Lutheran University in 1986, but an unexpected pregnancy caused Korah to put her collegiate career on hold the following year. This was the only aspect of their relationship Devin was not pleased with. But rather than desert her, he made a vow to always be there for Korah and their son. By then she trusted him fully. Even as a young man, Devin had the integrity and work ethics of a man twice his age.

He and Korah married in 1990, which was a big year for a number of reasons. That was the year Devin graduated with a degree in Construction Management, and it was also the year he founded the family business, Texas Builders. Success was not immediate, but it was also never in doubt – as far as Korah was concerned. The young couple welcomed their second child into the world in 1995. This time it was a girl. Devin named her Stephanie.

The next few years were filled with so many blessings, Korah forgot how precious each moment was until tragedy visited the Stewart household in 2001. A routine physical revealed an abnormality on Devin Sr.'s prostate gland. Further tests concluded the prostate gland was enlarged, cancer was the cause, and it had already spread to his colon and lymph nodes.

There wasn't much light for Korah in those gloomy days. The only thing she was thankful for was that the disease didn't prolong Devin's suffering. They fought the cancer with an aggressive regimen of surgery and chemotherapy. Devin was upbeat and courageous, but he lost the battle within five months of the original diagnosis. Korah became a widow at the tender age of 33.

Depression and despair never had a chance to take a foothold in her life, however, because Korah still had children to raise, and allowing her late husband's legacy to die with him was never an option. Prior to his death, Devin Sr. spent most of his time in the hospital training Korah to be the best unlicensed contractor the state had ever known. At times she became upset with him, urging him to put his business ledgers away and focus his energy on his recovery. But Devin would have none of that.

"Baby, please listen to me," he told her, on more than one occasion, while stretched out on a hospital bed at Jackson Memorial. "Texas Builders is my life, and it must not end with me. You can keep this thing rolling. You have to try your best."

It became increasingly hard to maintain focus, but Korah wiped the tears from her eyes and absorbed everything he taught her. After Devin's death, Korah returned to school to complete her higher education. Initially she wanted to be an English teacher, but she changed her major and graduated two years later with a degree in Construction Management, just like Devin.

Korah got her license and fulfilled her promise to not only keep the family business operational, but she also expanded Texas Builders much sooner than her late husband's projected goals. She would forever give Devin Sr. all of the credit for everything Texas Builders had become, but their vice president, Mrs. Priscilla Levin, was solely responsible for keeping the business afloat in the two years following his death. She taught Korah more about the construction game than any of her college professors, and Priscilla made sure the main office remained open throughout Devin's illness and Korah's time in school.

Each day that Korah showed up for work and saw Priscilla sitting behind her desk was a great day. She offered her the CEO position many times over the years, but Priscilla was content with running the show from behind the scenes.

Korah was currently training her nineteen year old daughter, Stephanie, to take Priscilla's place, but everyone knew that Priscilla was irreplaceable. Her expected retirement was something no one in the office wanted to accept or even consider.

Korah arrived at her office after nine a.m., which was late by her standards. But she was the boss, and technically she could get there any time she very well pleased. Unlike many of the other contracting companies in the state, Korah's front office was run entirely by women. That was totally coincidental, but it was also something she couldn't help but take a little pride in.

Korah had taken over her late husband's role as owner and CEO. Priscilla was the best vice president the construction game had ever known. Yolanda was Korah's personal assistant, and Stephanie was the company's administrative assistant. As with Devin, Korah assured her daughter that she did not have to get involved with the family business, but Stephanie never had a goal that didn't involve Texas Builders. She was currently studying construction at Texas Christian University.

Korah was greeted with appreciation and warmth that felt very familial as she headed for her corner office.

"Morning, Ms. Stewart!" Yolanda called.

"Hey, Mama!" Stephanie said.

"Korah, I am so excited!" Priscilla said.

Within seconds all three employees had entered her office. Korah took a seat behind her desk and looked up at them with a broad smile.

"Good morning, ladies! Nice to see everyone in such a good mood on a Monday."

Priscilla took a seat in the chair directly across from Korah, and Stephanie sat down in the only other chair in the room. She rolled it close to her mother's desk and continued to grin at her.

Korah reached and brushed a few stray hairs away from her daughter's eyes. Stephanie was beautiful. She had rich, smooth skin like Korah, and she had her mother's smarts and drive as well. Stephanie was short and pleasingly plump. She wore bold-rimmed glasses, and she always dressed smartly.

Priscilla was Jewish with long, dark hair and stylish reading glasses that were typically parked on the tip of her nose. She was always dressed modestly, with long dresses and pumps, and she preferred pearls over diamonds.

Korah's personal assistant, Yolanda, stood in the doorway cradling her iPad. She was the most beautiful of the crew, with long, sensual legs she chose to show off with skirts on most days. Yolanda was brown-skinned. Her long hair was braided this morning and wrapped up in a professional bun. She never needed more than a scant coat of lipstick to accentuate her perfect lips and teeth. Nearly every man who had cause to stop by the office found themselves growing enamored with Yolanda, including Korah's own son Devin Jr.

"I can't believe we're this close," Priscilla said. She rubbed her hands in her lap anxiously.

"I can't either," Korah said. "How do we know? I know they're pretty tight-lipped about the whole process."

"I found out," Stephanie said with a hint of pride. "I talked to Anthony last night, and he told me."

Although Korah lived less than 30 miles away from the university, her daughter opted to live on campus, so she would be immersed in the true college experience. Korah hated to see her go, but she was all for the decision.

Stephanie was currently a freshman, and she already had her first college crush. Interestingly, Anthony's mother just happened to be the secretary for the school district's superintendent. Stephanie's relationship with Anthony wasn't enough for the superintendent's decision to be biased, but it was enough for Korah and her crew to get an inside scoop about which bids were at the top of the list.

"When did he tell you that?" Korah asked.

"Last night," Stephanie beamed. "His parents invited me to dinner yesterday."

Korah raised an eyebrow, still smiling. "Really? How was it?"

"Awesome," Stephanie said. "Mrs. Rangel is a great cook. She made meatloaf and cabbage and cornbread."

"Wow, that sounds nice," Korah said. She knew that Stephanie had only been dating the superintendent's secretary's son for a couple of months. "Was that your first time meeting his folks?"

"Actually it was the second time they invited me over," Stephanie said.

"Anthony must talk about you a lot," Korah ventured.

Stephanie blushed.

"Um, what about the bid?" Yolanda asked from the doorway.

"I'm getting to that," Korah said. "But it's not every day that my little girl gets invited to meet her boyfriend's parents. This is a big deal."

"The bid is a big deal too, Mama," Stephanie said. "We're about to be in the big league."

Korah tried her best to slow her beating heart. She still didn't want to get her hopes up – no matter how promising things looked. "Okay, how did our company come up?" she finally asked.

"Anthony told his parents about you already," Stephanie reported. "While we were eating dinner, Mrs. Rangel said, 'So, Stephanie, I understand your mother owns Texas Builders...' I was nervous at first, because I didn't know what she was going to say. But then she smiled and said, 'We've heard great things about them. Your mother offered a bid for the new school we're building.'"

"Oh, Jesus." Korah clasped her hands together over her mouth. Her elbows rested on her desk.

"What's wrong, Mama?"

"I don't know if I want to hear this," Korah said. "You're giving me the shakes."

Stephanie laughed. "I told you it's good news."

Priscilla's smile confirmed this.

"I know, but it's a lot to handle," Korah admitted. "I can't believe she talked to you about it so candidly."

"She didn't," Stephanie said. "But I asked Anthony about it after we got back to school. He said his mom told him we're in the top two. He said it was probably going to be us or Brick House Construction."

Korah closed her eyes and exhaled slowly. She wished Devin Sr. could be there at that moment. She wished he could feel what she was feeling right now. But then she had to catch herself. She got over-excited before, and sometimes it didn't end well.

"Who's Brick House Construction?" she asked.

Yolanda approached with her iPad. "Here they are." She handed the device to the boss.

Korah stared down at the screen and then frowned in confusion. "What is this?"

"That's Brick House Construction," Yolanda said with a snicker. "That's their website."

Korah's smile became curious. "What is this?" she asked again. "This looks like an Abercrombie and Fitch ad."

Yolanda shook her head, grinning knowingly. "Nope. That's them."

Korah stared at the tablet in more detail. The website Yolanda had pulled up was clearly for Brick House Construction. But rather than their logo or one of their constructions or simply links to the appropriate pages, there was a huge photo of a man covering the top half of the screen. He was wearing jeans and a white button-down and a *cowboy hat* – a Stetson. He was leaning against a wrought iron gate that was part of a beautiful entryway to the majestic Avery Ranch. Korah knew the name of the ranch because it was mounted above the gate in dark, iron lettering.

The cowboy was black and strikingly handsome, rough and rugged. His skin was caramel colored, his face clean-shaven, his jawline hard and rigid. He had a serious expression. The way he stared at the camera gave Korah an unexpected chill. Behind him, she could see the ranch, which was stunning, but it seemed to pale in comparison to its apparent owner.

On the bottom right portion of the photo, Korah saw the words

Brock "Brick" Avery
CEO Brick House Construction
Pure Texan

Korah's mouth was hanging open by the time she looked up from the iPad. She stared at Yolanda, unable to articulate the thoughts in her head.

Stephanie leaned over to get a better look, and her eyes widened as well.

"He's a looker, ain't he?" Yolanda offered.

"I'm not worried about what he looks like," Korah managed. "I just can't believe this is their actual website. Seems a little..."

"Caught your eye, though. Didn't it?" Yolanda said.

Korah rolled her eyes at that.

"They're the real deal," Yolanda told her. "They've built a lot of nice properties – and even a school."

Korah's hopes were instantly dashed. Her company had never built a school. That was one of the reasons this job was so important.

"I can't believe this Brock guy has his picture this big on the front page of their website," Korah said, looking at the iPad again. "That's what he wants to lead with – his..." Her eyebrows bunched as she was forced to acknowledge the obvious. "...his, *good looks*? He should call himself *Prick* instead of Brick." She chuckled at her own joke.

But it wasn't funny, and she knew it. Prick Avery might take her dream job! Korah already hated his stupid, handsome face.

"Looks aren't everything," Priscilla said, hoping to regain some of the enthusiasm Yolanda's iPad took away. "The superintendent's people are looking at numbers, not his picture."

"I know," Korah grumbled. "But if he's built a school, he's already got an advantage over us." She finally clicked the link that showed off some of his properties and renovations. Every set of photos turned the day into just another dumb Monday.

"We're still in the top two," Stephanie said. "Maybe if his bid is too high, they'll go with the company with the lower bid, even if we're not as established."

"We're just as good as Brick House," Yolanda argued. "They're impressive, but they can't do anything we can't do."

"That's right," Priscilla said, and Korah's heart dared to beat quickly again.

"If all else fails, maybe Stephanie can nag Anthony so much, he'll make his mom suggest you," Yolanda said with a grin.

"I can do that," Stephanie readily agreed.

"No, please don't," Korah said, shaking her head.

"I was just kidding," Yolanda said.

"I'm not," Stephanie said. She was brimming with excitement over her new task. "I can work on Anthony. Like, for *real*. I'm ready to take one for the team!"

Her smile faded when she saw the look of revulsion her mom fixed on her.

"I wasn't talking about *sex*, Mama," Stephanie said, reading her mind. "Dang. Get your mind out the gutter." She smiled coyly.

Brick House is on sale now. Learn more about this book and my other titles at keithwalkerbooks.com

ABOUT THE AUTHOR

Keith Thomas Walker, known as the Master of Romantic Suspense and Urban Fiction, is the author of nearly two dozen novels, including *Life After, The Realest Ever,* the *Brick House* series and the *Finley High* series. Keith's books transcend all genres. He has published romance, urban fiction, mystery/thriller, teen/young adult, Christian, poetry and erotica. Originally from Fort Worth, he is a graduate of Texas Wesleyan University. Keith has won or been nominated for numerous awards in the categories of "Best Male Author," "Best Romance," "Best Urban Fiction," "Best Young Adult Romance," and "Author of the Year," from several book clubs and organizations. Visit him at www.keithwalkerbooks.com.

www.ingramcontent.com/pod-product-compliance
Lightning Source LLC
Chambersburg PA
CBHW030647110726
47901CB00002B/597